Dear Reader,

If you've picked up this book you've fallen under the spell of Harlequin Blaze's Uniformly Hot! miniseries. There's something irresistible about a warrior, a man who puts duty and honor first. I was so drawn to these heroes, I wrote two books about air force fighter pilots. *Obsessed? Me?*

In *All the Right Moves,* Captain John Devlin is at a crossroads. It's time for him to sign up for his second tour, though he's torn about staying in the military. He's had a fantastic offer to pilot a luxury private plane, a job that would give him freedom and a first-class ticket to see the world. He's not even sure why the magic seems to have gone from the only job he's ever loved.

Then he meets Cassie O'Brien. She's a quirky beauty who wants nothing to do with fighter jocks. She's a serious grad student who spends most of her time tending bar, but only until she finishes school.

Soon John and Cassie are burning up the sheets and spending every free minute together. Could it be that the one thing missing from his ideal life had nothing to do with flying, and everything to do with the woman he flew home to? And would Cassie even want to become part of a fighter jock's life?

Check out *To the Limit* in August, where former fighter pilot Sam Brody finds himself falling for the young widow of an old friend as he struggles to make a new life after he's lost his wings.

All my best,

Jo Leigh

All the Right Moves

Jo Leigh

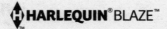

HHARLEQUIN® BLAZE™

Recycling programs
for this product may
not exist in your area.

ISBN-13: 978-0-373-79756-1

ALL THE RIGHT MOVES

Copyright © 2013 by Jolie Kramer

This edition published by arrangement with Harlequin Books S.A.

For questions and comments about the quality of this book, please contact us at CustomerService@Harlequin.com.

Printed in U.S.A.

ABOUT THE AUTHOR

Jo Leigh is from Los Angeles and always thought she'd end up living in Manhattan. So how did she end up in Utah, in a tiny town with a terrible internet connection, being bossed around by a housefull of rescued cats and dogs? What the heck, she says, predictability is boring. Jo has written more than forty-five novels for Harlequin Books. Visit her website at www.joleigh.com or contact her at joleigh@joleigh.com.

Books by Jo Leigh

HARLEQUIN BLAZE

To get the inside scoop on Harlequin Blaze and its talented writers, be sure to check out blazeauthors.com.

Other titles by this author available in ebook format. Don't miss any of our special offers. Write to us at the following address for information on our newest releases.

Harlequin Reader Service
U.S.: 3010 Walden Ave., P.O. Box 1325, Buffalo, NY 14269
Canadian: P.O. Box 609, Fort Erie, Ont. L2A 5X

To all the military heroes among us,
and their families.
Thank you for your service.

1

WITH THE TEMPERATURE hovering near a hundred, John Devlin climbed out of his new Corvette into the unrelenting Vegas heat, locked the car and pocketed his keys. The June sun was so brutal he considered parking closer to the market, but he dismissed the idea in a heartbeat. That was the trouble with owning an expensive sports car. You avoided dings even if it meant walking half a mile. Worth it, though, for the honey of a silver Corvette.

Any inconvenience was an acceptable trade-off because John was all about speed. In the air or on the ground, it didn't matter, damn it. That had a much better ring than having a midlife crisis at thirty-three.

He crossed the asphalt and slipped off his Wayfarers just as the store's automatic doors opened. Man, he did not like grocery shopping. Good thing he only had to do it twice a month, and only when he wasn't deployed.

His grocery list rarely varied so he headed straight for the liquor aisle, grabbed a bottle of Lagavulin scotch, then moved on to the middle rows where he picked up a box of crackers and a loaf of bread. The blonde—he was pretty sure her name was Megan—behind the deli counter spotted him and smiled.

"Hey, Captain Devlin." She had to be in high school, or barely out, but she gave him a once-over like a pro. Girls grew up fast these days. "A pound of turkey, sliced thin?"

"You know me so well."

Her practiced smile said *not well enough,* which he ignored by studying the cheese selection. One time he'd stopped in wearing his flight suit and it had been Captain Devlin ever since. Nice to be anonymous sometimes, though being stationed at a base the size of Nellis, it wasn't easy. He might as well have stopped at the commissary.

"You want a half pound of sliced Muenster, too?" she asked, her voice close.

He looked up to find her leaning with one hand against the glass case and checking out the front of his jeans. Jesus. "Yeah, Muenster. Thanks. I'll be back for it."

Not sure his mayo was still good, he headed down the condiment aisle, snagging a jar of green olives along the way. The Cold Beer sign caught his attention. He was officially on leave so why not? He managed to grab a six-pack without dropping everything. Barely. But he still had stuff to pick up. Sighing, he gave in and went in search of a basket. He found one near the express register and piled in his groceries.

The thought of returning to the deli counter was not a pleasant one. At the back of the store he stopped for a quart of cream and checked to see if Megan had set his order on the counter. Looking bored she stood at the meat slicer, pushing the blade back and forth, probably still working on his turkey. However, a well-dressed middle-aged woman studying the food in the glass made it safer to approach. She tapped her foot, gave him a cool glance, then looked at her watch.

If she wasn't a military wife, he'd eat his boot. Coolly elegant even if the thermometer hit 120. They didn't ruffle easily, could be ready to move halfway across the world on a moment's notice and manage to throw a dinner party the night after they arrived. But get in their way? He'd never met a more determined bunch than air force wives needing to get a move on.

He ended up checking his own watch, although he couldn't blame the woman. It felt weird being in a grocery store in the middle of the day. He was used to his routine, even if the routine was completely contingent on a dozen factors he had no control over. Still, for every flight there was mission planning, prebriefing, flying time, sortie, debriefing, qweep—all the soul-sucking paperwork—and ground ops. Never a dull moment, as they say.

Given that his time was his own for the next ten days, there was only one thing on his agenda. He had a decision to make. One that would impact the rest of his life.

"Here you go, Captain Devlin." Megan was smiling, leaning into the case and holding out his order. Her lips were red. They hadn't been earlier. "Anything else?"

"That'll do it. Thanks." John nodded at the older woman, who'd slid him a curious look. "Ma'am," he said, dropping the packages into his basket and turning to leave.

"See you in a couple of weeks," Megan called after him.

He lifted a hand without looking back.

In two weeks it could be a whole new ball game for him. He might be receiving new orders to test the latest in the F-35 series of jets, an assignment he'd wanted his entire career, or he could be shopping for a civilian wardrobe and learning everything there was to know about the Gulfstream 650. The worst of it was he didn't know which fork he'd be taking. Not even a hint. His dependable decisiveness had gone AWOL. For maybe the first time in his life, he didn't know what the hell he wanted to do.

He paid for his groceries, anxious to get behind the wheel of the 'Vette, not so anxious to be at the mercy of the desert heat. But when he stepped outside and heard the familiar roar of a Raptor overhead, there was nothing to do but stop, slip on his sunglasses and look up at the sky.

The Raptor was a thing of beauty, ascending into the clear blue heavens. Even after studying four years at the Air Force Academy and nearly eleven of active service he still got a rush watching a bird slicing through the sky. These days it was the most excitement he experienced on the ground.

Sitting in a cockpit was a different story. Strapped in and moving fast over the world he always felt alive and focused. It was when he came back to earth that things had gotten confusing. Something was…off. If he didn't know better, he'd say that being a pilot wasn't the end-all, be-all of his life. But of course it was. Everything he did, in or out of uniform, was preparation to take the controls. Everything.

He watched the contrail begin to dissipate, then

moved toward his car. As soon as he pulled out of the parking lot he had the urge to press the accelerator, but that would have to wait. Too much traffic, and it would be slow going all the way to his condo near the Strip.

After an irritating twenty minutes of crawling behind a truck to his high-rise, John got his groceries put away in record time. Considered, then rejected, having a scotch while he checked email on his iPhone. The place smelled lemony, his cue that the housekeeper had been by. Couldn't tell by the looks of things. He wasn't home much. He didn't get a lot of junk mail or magazines or papers. Mostly because all his mail went directly to his sister in Seattle. She paid his bills out of a joint checking account, which was a real lifesaver when he was overseas.

He flipped on the flat-screen TV hanging on the wall. The remote in one hand and his phone in the other, he moved to the massive glass window with a view of the Strip. At night it was very cool with all the lights and flash. This afternoon the brown tinges of smog hanging over the valley just depressed him.

With his focus on his phone screen, he aimed the remote at the TV behind him and flipped to ESPN. He had an email from Lauren, instructing him to deduct the cable bill she'd just paid, and letting him know his two nephews were nagging for a call or visit. That one was tough. He wasn't anxious to talk to the family right now. He'd rather they didn't know he was on leave or be reminded he was up for reenlistment.

They'd be appalled he was even considering ending his military career. Especially his father. John didn't want to think about having that kind of discussion with the colonel. The old man would probably have a heart attack. But then his father had been damn lucky. During his thirty years of service he'd never lost a close buddy....

Hell, this wasn't about Danny's death. Or Sam being grounded, his career as an active duty F-16 pilot ripped away because of something beyond his control.

If the restlessness driving John crazy had anything to do with either of his friends, he'd admit it. No problem. He wasn't trying to be the strong silent type. It was not knowing what was wrong that had him tied in knots. For all he knew, he'd wake up in a couple of months and everything would be A-OK. Trouble was, he didn't have a couple of months. He needed to commit or get off the pot before this new downsized air force decided it could live without his services. Or before Tony Wagner, one of the richest men in America, got impatient and rescinded his offer to make John his private pilot.

He looked toward McCarran Airport and saw a commercial jet taking off. Leave at home was always disconcerting. Not going to the base made him feel vaguely anxious. No doubt he'd end up stopping by at some point. He'd see the guys over the next ten days. A few of his buddies were meeting for dinner and then clubhopping tomorrow night and then there was the party at Shane's house coming up.

What to do now was the problem. He didn't feel like TV or drinking alone or doing much of anything. Except driving. He hadn't given the Corvette a good run yet. Slipping his phone into his pocket, he turned off the TV, then grabbed his keys from the kitchen counter.

He'd head out to the desert and find a nice long stretch of road. And hope he avoided a speeding ticket.

"I NEED ANOTHER PITCHER. Oh, and two frosted mugs."

Cassie O'Brien looked up from the textbook she had stashed by the plate of cut-up limes, and squinted at Lisa, then toward the pool tables at the back of the bar. "Who's asking for fresh mugs?"

"Pete and Lou." The waitress made a face. "Sorry. You need me to wash glasses?"

Cassie sighed. "No, but I wouldn't mind you turning down the volume," she said, glancing up at the speaker hanging from the wall between the Grateful Dead and Sugarland Express posters.

Good thing she didn't have a gun hidden under the bar or she'd be tempted to shoot the damn jukebox. She didn't exactly hate country music, and she didn't even mind when the tunes got loud. But it was hell trying to study with all that racket.

"*Your brother* needs to hire another person for times like this." Lisa eyed the psychology textbook as she dragged a chair under the speaker, then climbed up on it. "You should find someone willing to work odd shifts. He doesn't know what's going on around here half the time anyway."

It wasn't so much Lisa's snippy tone but how she'd referred to Tom that tipped off Cassie that the lovebirds had had another fight. There was no doubt it was Tommy's fault. She loved her brother. She did. But ever since he'd come back from Iraq he'd been tough to deal with, and unfortunately, Lisa suffered the brunt of his slippery moods. Cassie understood his bitterness, everyone did. But Lisa had stuck by him through months of rehab, filling in when Cassie couldn't. Lisa loved Tommy, but the big dope was so caught up in his past he couldn't see what was staring him in the face now.

Cassie was going to have a long-overdue talk with him. But first she had to seriously crack the books and take her three final exams. Not just take them, ace the suckers. The job market was too tight for an average grad student to expect to land anything decent. And dear God, she didn't want to be a bartender her whole life. Or even by the time she hit thirty in two very short years.

In a week exams would be over and she would be able to breathe again.

At least until her final two classes started in September. Once she finished, then just maybe she'd find a real job before she was eligible to collect social security.

"Is that good?" Lisa asked, one hand hovering near the speaker's volume control, the other flattened to the wall to steady the wobbly chair.

"Perfect." Cassie wiped her hands on the towel hanging over her shoulder and held the chair until Lisa climbed down. "Thank you. Here's your pitcher and fresh mugs." She pushed the tray toward Lisa, blew at the annoying loose curl that had escaped her ponytail and leaned over the bar so she could be heard in the back. "Everyone hang on to your mugs. The dishwasher is broken."

"I'll come wash your glasses, you sweet thing." It was Spider. "Wouldn't want your pretty little hands to get shriveled up."

Cassie and Lisa both shook their heads at the raucous

laughter coming from his fellow pool players, most of them veteran bikers like Spider. She let him get away with more than most because he was old enough to be her father. In fact he'd ridden with her parents and the Diablo Outlaws for a few years when she was a toddler.

"I imagine you have your own shrinkage to worry about," she shot back, exchanging grins with Lisa, who picked up her tray and headed for the back.

A chorus of "whoas" couldn't drown out Spider's laugh. He was a scary-looking dude with a long shaggy beard and a dozen fading tats trailing up his beefy arms and the side of his neck. But inside he was a teddy bear. She'd heard he hadn't always been like that. He'd mellowed with age and a short prison sentence, and she was just fine with not knowing the details.

She looked around the room, recognizing every customer but one. That was how it usually worked at the Gold Strike, ever since Tommy bought the place and she'd started bartending here two years ago. A few unfamiliar strays came in throughout the week, some stayed and became regulars, the rest she never saw again.

What she liked best was the diverse mix of military vets, aging bikers, university students and staff from the nearby hospital who frequented the bar. They were a friendly lot, though they didn't all know each other by name. Occasionally a few airmen from Nellis stopped in, and if it happened that college women were hanging around that day, she was likely to see the same guys again.

But the Gold Strike wasn't close enough to the base to attract many active servicemen. At one time the place had been a hard-core biker bar on the outskirts of Las

Vegas. When the growing popularity of the city meant residential and business areas kept spreading farther and farther out, the bikers finally said adios. Turned out to be a good deal for Tommy.

"Hey, Cassie." Pete came from the back and slid onto a stool, leaned forward, swept back a stubborn lock of brown hair and stared at her with serious dark eyes. She knew he was twenty-one but he seemed so young she wanted to card him every time he walked in. "Help me out with something," he said in a low, nervous voice while casting a cautious look toward the pool tables.

"If I can." She braced her elbows on the bar and leaned over so no one else could hear. "What's up?"

"I'm making dinner for this girl. I've only been out with her once so I wanna impress her." He swallowed, his Adam's apple bobbing in his thin neck. But his voice creaked from dry mouth and he kept sweeping stealthy looks toward the back. "I wanna buy wine, but I don't know what kind or how much I gotta spend."

Cassie filled a glass with water and set it in front of him. This was normal. For some reason people treated her like an information booth. No question was out of bounds, even though the regulars kept trying to stump her or embarrass her, but she never minded. "Does she drink red or white?"

Pete's eyes narrowed. "How many kinds are there?"

"Do you know if she even drinks wine?"

His lips spread in a boyish grin. "I figure she does. She's older." He lifted his chin at a cocksure angle that he probably assumed was macho, and that she really wanted to tell him not to do. "Twenty-three, I think."

"Ah." Cassie got herself some water. "Do you know how to cook?"

"Yeah." Pete shrugged a shoulder, his chin making a sharp descent toward the bar. "What do you mean?"

She would not laugh, no matter what. "What are you planning to make for dinner?"

"I mean, I can probably follow a recipe." He drummed his fingers on the ancient scarred oak Cassie tried to keep polished. "You have a suggestion?"

"I do." She picked up his hand. "First, get the grease out from under your fingernails. Seriously. I know you work on cars for a living, but this is a major turnoff."

He blushed a little, withdrawing his hand, but didn't argue. He knew the rule, all the customers did. They could ask her anything. But they had to be prepared for an honest answer.

"And don't try to cook. It's hotter than hell. Take her someplace—better than McDonalds," she added, and he rolled his eyes. "Then when it cools off, go for a moonlit walk along Lake Mead. Drink a beer or two in the car. It's illegal but only if you get caught." She winked. "Don't try so hard. If it happens, it happens. Just don't bring her here."

Pete almost choked on his water. He used the back of his arm to wipe the dribble on his chin and glanced at his pool buddies, the merciless bunch. "No way."

She grinned. "Now get out of here. I'm trying to study."

He hopped off the stool. "You want me to wash this glass?"

"No. Go." She motioned with a tilt of her head, but her gaze went to the front door when she heard it open.

It was her brother. Sitting in his wheelchair, rolling down the handicap ramp into the room.

Damn him.

Lisa walked up with her empty tray pressed to her hip and gave him the scathing look he deserved. She didn't say a word, just turned and placed the tray on the bar so that only Cassie could see the hurt and disappointment in her blue eyes.

Unshaven, his collar-length hair poking out in search of a comb, Tommy didn't bother to acknowledge them as he passed and started to wheel himself toward the back.

"Hold it." Cassie stepped out from behind the bar, prepared to stop him if he didn't respond.

But he knew better, and reluctantly wheeled around to look at her. "What?"

If the word hadn't come out surly she might have felt more than a tug of sympathy. He was her big brother. Only two years older, yet he'd been as protective of her as a mother bear with her cub throughout their nomadic childhood going from one biker camp to the next. And she in turn had protected him in every way she knew how. But an IED on an isolated Iraqi road had taken his leg and changed him down to the core, leaving this wounded, antagonistic stranger. She wasn't about to give up on him. No one who loved him could.

"Why are you in the chair?" she asked, blocking him so he couldn't bolt to his buddies in the back.

"You know why."

"If I did, would I be asking?" Her gaze fell to the T-shirt she'd given him for his birthday. "Your shirt is inside out."

He looked down at the words *Life is Good* and laughed. Raising hazel eyes that were identical to her own, he blew out a sharp breath. "The leg chafes."

"You had it refitted two weeks ago."

"It still isn't right," he muttered, careful not to glance at Lisa.

"How come it only chafes when you're feeling sorry for yourself?" Cassie held his gaze.

"Go practice your psychology bullshit on someone else." He cursed under his breath.

Lisa turned and gave him another sour look before going to check on her tables.

"What's her problem?"

"Gee, I don't have to be a psychologist to figure that one out." Cassie went back behind the bar before she said something she regretted. Part of this was her fault. She'd coddled him too much in the beginning. And when he'd bought the bar, she'd taken on the lion's share of the responsibility, hoping like hell he'd find his strength in building something of his own. But it had been two years now, and he was still depressed, still stubbornly refusing medication or continued therapy. Unfortunately, she knew all too well that he needed to *want* to get better. If Lisa, who'd stuck with him through the worst of times, couldn't get him there, what chance did Cassie have?

"You gonna pour me a beer while I go change this shirt?" He gave her a small smile, half apology, half don't-be-mad-at-me.

That was the trouble. Maybe if she stayed angry with him long enough for him to grow up, get some counseling, they'd both be better off. He knew she had exams.

He should've been prepared to cover for her tonight so she could study. But that wouldn't happen. Not with him in the chair. Instead he'd spend the evening hiding from life and throwing darts with his friends.

And she'd pretend everything was going to be okay. "Yeah, I'll get your beer." She reached for a mug, watched him start to wheel away and decided not to let him off scot-free. "I'll have Lisa bring it to you."

He hesitated, his gloved hands still on the wheel rims, then without looking back, he shoved off, continuing toward the pool tables.

God, it made her sad to see him sitting in that damn chair. He should be upright, walking, doing things he hadn't been able to do for two years. He hated the limp, but jeez, he was so lucky. He was alive. He was his own boss, he had people who cared about him. Although she'd never had to face anything that huge, so...

She streamed beer from the tap into his mug as Lisa came up to the bar. She looked defeated. Sad. If she gave up on Tom for good, Cassie wouldn't blame her. Not even a little.

"Gordon wants another gin and tonic." Lisa sagged against the bar. "Two more drafts for Mickey and Leroy, with shots."

"My brother's a first-class jerk."

"Yes, he is."

"Mind taking him his beer?"

"Can't promise I won't dump it over his head."

Cassie smiled. "Might do him some good."

"Sure couldn't hurt." The door opened and they both turned. "Holy...shit," Lisa murmured. "Ever see him before?"

Cassie shook her head and quickly looked away. Tall, maybe six feet, dark hair slightly longer than a military cut, great body—the guy was too hot for his own good, and she wasn't about to be one of those silly women who stared.

From her peripheral vision, she saw him take a seat at the end of the bar. She turned her head for just another quick peek and met his whiskey-brown eyes.

2

"A FLYBOY, HUH?"

"Yep." Cassie concentrated on the gin and tonic she was making, but almost forgot the lime wedge.

"What do you think, a captain? Major?"

"Captain."

"Fast movers?"

"Please." Cassie snorted. "Any doubt?"

"He won't stick around long."

"Nope.

"A damn shame." Lisa was trying to be inconspicuous and failing. "I could stare at him all night."

"You're off to a good start," Cassie murmured quietly, then darted him a look. "I'll be right with you."

"Take your time."

"Oh, my God, that smile, that voice." Lisa sighed.

Cassie had turned away so fast she'd missed the smile. "So much for Tommy."

"Screw him."

"Don't blame you there. Go take Flyboy's order if you want. I'll finish your drinks."

"You sure?"

"Go for it."

Lisa glanced toward the back. "Then I'll take Tommy his beer. If he comes looking for it, he might scare off the best-looking customer we've had in six months."

Well, that was a headache Cassie didn't need. But Lisa was right. Tommy was fine with enlisted men and retirees, welcomed them, actually. But officers? He had no use for the whole lot of them. He wasn't necessarily confrontational, but he could make things uncomfortable.

Refusing to watch Lisa approach the dark-haired guy, Cassie kept her head down, making drinks, realizing too late she'd poured an extra tequila shot. A new doctor who'd worked in the E.R. at the hospital had started coming in a month ago. She'd only seen him a few times and he sure was easy on the eyes. But this pilot...he was something.

Still, she didn't go for the Jon Hamm types with the perfect movie-star looks, all cool and suave. As soon as they opened their mouths you had to wonder how their ego had fit through the door. Not all of them, but enough. Then again those types didn't go for her, either, so it all worked out.

"He wants a scotch. Neat." Smiling, Lisa loaded her tray. "Five bucks says he leaves after two sips."

"I'm so broke I can't afford to bet a quarter. Did you warn him this isn't a scotch kind of place?"

"Uh-uh. I didn't want him to leave that fast." Lisa picked up her tray and left to deliver the drinks.

Cassie dried her hands, then grabbed the bottle of scotch off the shelf. The only reason it wasn't dusty was because she kept a clean bar. She reached for a glass, unscrewed the bottle, then sighed. Recapping it, she walked over to the man, who was leaning back and watching her.

Up close he was even more dazzling. Dark, almost black hair. Tan skin. Some combination of eyebrows and jawline and mouth that made looking at him a sensual experience even if you didn't want it to be. But she didn't like the intense way he tracked her with those damn sexy eyes, so he lost a couple of points.

She held up the bottle so he could see the label. "This is all we have."

"Okay," he said with a slight frown.

"Are you familiar with the brand?"

"No."

"It probably sucks."

His laugh was short, surprised. "I'll take my chances."

Cassie hated returning points to the plus column but to be fair, the humor in his expression made him look even hotter. "Just remember I warned you," she said, turning back to get the glass and to pull herself together. She hadn't expected him to be such a good sport.

Lisa returned to pick up Tommy's beer. "What was that?" she asked under her breath.

"I gave him an out on the scotch but he passed." She poured a generous portion. If he could stomach the stuff, he deserved the extra booze. "You can take it over to him."

"No, go ahead. You seem to be doing just fine with him."

"Right." The only reason she didn't roll her eyes was because he was still watching her. What did he think she was going to do, spit in his drink? "Do me a favor. Don't go overboard giving Tommy a hard time. I don't want to deal with one of his moods today."

Lisa went toward the back, and Cassie took the scotch to the flyboy at the other end of the bar. She almost forgot to set down a cocktail napkin because she didn't bother for most of their customers. They generally ignored them once they picked up their drink.

"Here you go." She set the glass on the plain white paper square. "That'll be three bucks."

"Can I start a tab?"

"Really?"

"I'll give you a credit card if you're worried I'll run out on you." That damn smile... How many tight spots had it gotten him out of?

"I'd try the scotch first," she said, leaning back and folding her arms across her chest. She couldn't have worn a worse T-shirt. Faded, too snug, it had some geeky cartoon character on the front. But it was a freebie and that fit into her clothes budget just fine.

He took a sip, not a cautious one, either. He blinked, swallowed, then slowly nodded, his gaze staying on the amber liquid.

She grinned, got that weird feeling someone was watching her and caught Gordon's eye from across the room. A quick glare told him to mind his own business, but the customers at the two other occupied tables were keeping tabs, too, so it didn't matter.

Cassie straightened, but it wasn't as if she were doing anything wrong. She was friendly with all her customers. "Well?"

Clearing his throat, he slid the glass toward her. "I think I'll take a beer."

"I have plenty of that. What kind?"

"Whatever's on tap."

"You sure? We have the imported stuff."

"Tap is fine. What about food?"

She picked up the scotch, frowning at him. Okay, now he was just messing with her. "What about it?"

"Uh…" His eyebrows went up and there was no missing the amusement in his brown eyes. "Do you serve any?"

Was he crazy? If they did, would he eat in a place like this? "We have pretzels for sure, maybe some peanuts. On the house, but that's it."

She moved back to her station. As much as she hated to admit it, looking directly into his eyes sparked something inside her that was unsettling. It wasn't as if she thought the sensation meant anything. He wasn't just an eleven out of ten, he seemed nice, and she kind of wished he wasn't. It was so much easier to ignore the ones who were full of themselves.

Cassie found the pretzels right away because she'd put out bowls earlier for the guys in the back. Sadly, she had only three clean mugs left. Sighing, she grabbed one and stuck it under the spout, started a slow stream of beer, then stretched over to the sink and turned on the hot water.

What the hell was taking Lisa so long? Cassie would need her help before the hospital changed shifts and customers piled in. The beer foamed over the mug, and she tipped it to get rid of some of the head. She'd already given him rotgut scotch. She didn't want to replace it with froth.

She stopped to add dish detergent to the water, then carried his pretzels and beer to him. "If you still want a tab I'll start one. I'm not charging you for the scotch."

"Yes, you are." His dark brows dipped. "You warned me. Fair is fair."

She set down the draft, and he touched her hand, though she didn't think he meant to. But she would've missed the cocktail napkin if he hadn't moved it to accommodate her. The skin around her knuckles was dry and unattractive from washing too many glasses without gloves, and she hated that she noticed. What she did like was that he insisted on paying for the scotch. Even her regulars tried to mooch free beer.

"So? A tab?" She slid the pretzels toward him, keeping her gaze on the tables.

"Yep."

"All righty, then." Turning to get her pad at the other end, she dragged her palms down the front of her jeans.

"Wait."

"Yeah?"

"What do you have going on back there besides pool?"

She hesitated, hoping he didn't decide to go poking around. Spider and his gang wouldn't cause trouble. They might make an off-color remark, but only in fun. It was Tommy she didn't trust. "Intrigue. Desperate deeds. Things that would shock you to your soul."

"Really?"

"Or as we like to call it, darts. And barely enough

room for the gang of mechanics that took it over an hour ago. Sorry."

"Damn. I was primed for danger." The corners of his mouth twitched as if he knew she was trying to discourage him.

"Boy, have you picked the wrong bar." She smiled, knowing she wouldn't see him again.

"What's your name?"

"Cassie." She noticed how his long tanned fingers fit all the way around the mug. He had nice hands, clean, trimmed nails. "The waitress is Lisa if you want another beer and can't get my attention."

"You'll get that busy?"

"Oh, yeah. Any minute now."

He glanced around the mostly empty room. "I'm John," he said as she headed back to her station. "For my tab."

She nodded without looking back. His smoky baritone was enough to fire up her nerve endings. She wondered if he'd given her his real name, or if it was one he used for pizza deliveries. *John* seemed too plain for a man who looked like him. She'd expected something more dashing, maybe an unusual family name.

She wrote down his beer, stashed the slip with the other two tabs beside the register and looked up just as Lisa returned from the back. She shook her head, the usual signal for "don't ask."

Then Cassie heard the door open, followed by a burst of voices and laughter. It was the hospital gang. Sighing, she closed her textbook and put it away, not looking forward to getting off work then spending the rest of the night studying.

JOHN HEARD THE VOICES, felt a blast of desert air at his back and turned. At first he'd thought someone had held the door open too long, but people kept coming inside the cool dim bar. The majority wore scrubs, a few still had their hospital IDs hanging from around their necks. Two guys went straight to Cassie while the others claimed three tables in the corner near the No Trespassing sign that hung on the wood-paneled wall.

He figured she'd been exaggerating that the place would get busy, that it was a ploy to get rid of him. He'd gotten the impression she didn't think he belonged here, and she wasn't wrong. The loud country music, hard metal posters, questionable bumper stickers plastered crookedly to the walls—none of it was his style. He'd seen the four Harleys parked outside, so he'd known beforehand this wouldn't exactly be an officer's club. Which had been the point.

He wasn't in the mood to do what he always did, expect what he always expected, talk to the same people he always talked to. Something had to shake him from his uncertainty. He'd thought about leaving Vegas, going somewhere crazy. Tahiti or Pittsburgh. But he didn't want to fly anywhere, not if he wasn't the pilot. So the next best thing was to change neighborhoods.

The door opened again. This time it was a thirty-something woman in civvies, who joined the group wearing scrubs. The older rough-looking guys who'd already been drinking when John came in seemed to know the newcomers, and there was a brief but polite exchange before everyone returned to the business of imbibing or ordering from the blonde waitress. Lisa, according to Cassie.

He wouldn't forget her name. It suited her. Not that he could say why. He didn't know a Cassie or a Cassandra that he recalled. But with those big hazel eyes, the smooth fair complexion and that sense of humor, the name seemed to fit. Her auburn hair was on the curly side, and she habitually blew at the loose tendrils that seemed to keep getting in her way.

Sipping his beer, he tried to figure out what cartoon was on the front of her T-shirt without being obvious. Her small compact body appealed to him and it would be easy to just stare. The fabric stretched tight across her breasts didn't help. It made him curious as to whether wearing the smaller size was by design, or if she just hadn't cared what she grabbed out of the drawer. Her faded jeans looked as if they'd been around awhile, and again, the snug fit made it difficult not to be one of those creepy guys he wouldn't wish on anyone.

Maybe she wore the tight clothes to bolster her tips. Although in a place like this no one was leaving anything extravagant. She was good with the customers, he'd give her that. She knew a lot of them by name, which was unusual in this town. It was also odd that the bar didn't have video poker and slot machines. Every place in Vegas had machines. Gas stations, supermarkets, diners. He'd figured a bar without the ability to lose a paycheck would be mostly empty, but the evidence proved him wrong.

He worked on his beer, less worried about staring at Cassie now that the place was so packed. Clearly she was well liked. People stopped to say hi or to ask her a question or tell a joke. She rolled her eyes at a bawdy riddle, then grinned and kept working, her hands plunged in sudsy water, while waiting for pitchers to fill with beer.

When a young woman in pink scrubs asked for pretzels, Cassie put her to work loading bowls for every table. Cassie herself stayed on task, juggling mixed-drink orders, keeping the draft flowing and carefully checking glasses she'd just washed.

She wasn't only attentive, she moved fast and was quick-witted. Maybe she owned the bar.

"Hey, Cassie."

Her head came up, her gaze going to someone in the corner. "Hey, what?"

"Where's the cheapest gas today?"

"The Pilot on Craig."

"Thanks." The man chuckled. "You owe me five bucks," he said to his companion, who started to argue about the accuracy of the information.

Several others booed him. An older man in a wheelchair with two mixed drinks in front of him swore Cassie was never wrong.

John hadn't given the guy more than a passing glance but now he noticed his ball cap. It read Retired Air Force. He'd finished his career a sergeant was John's guess. A permanent frown was etched on the old-timer's grizzled face, reminding John of Master Sergeant Henry Ludlow. The man had already put in his twenty by the time they'd met. John had been a young lieutenant, still green and way too cocky. It was Ludlow who'd whipped him into shape. The man had never disrespected John's rank but he sure hadn't taken his crap, either. Thinking back, he smiled.

"You okay over there?" Cassie's voice brought him around.

He checked his beer, surprised that he'd already downed half of it. "I'm good for now."

She nodded, a faint smile tugging at her lips as she turned her attention to the slip the waitress set in front of her.

He'd chosen the ideal stool at the end of the bar. Although if he moved over one she'd be in his line of sight at all times. At the moment he couldn't see her lower half. Just as well. He wasn't trolling. And even if he was, she wasn't giving him an interested vibe.

She did intrigue him, though. He wasn't accustomed to a woman trying to get rid of him, and now he was curious about the whole Q&A thing she had going on. Was she that knowledgeable? Or was it just a parlor trick? They sure hung on to her answers.

Using the back of her wrist to brush a curl off her flushed cheek, she looked up, her narrowed gaze panning the room. "All right, who ordered the piña colada?"

John glanced over his shoulder.

A hand slowly raised. With a wince, the last woman to come in said, "It's me, Cassie. But if it's too much trouble, that's okay."

"Oh, that's right. You just got back from Hawaii." Cassie thought for a moment, her lips pursed.

John stared too long at her lush mouth and had a reaction he wasn't prepared for. He shifted positions on the wooden bar stool. What the hell was wrong with him?

Cassie bent over and pulled out cans of tomato and

cranberry juice. "Sorry, Beth. I don't have all the ingredients."

"Never mind. Really. Make it my usual."

Cassie straightened. "I'll pick up the right mixes and you can have one the next time you come in."

"Please, don't worry about it. You have enough on your plate this month."

Cassie just smiled and went back to pouring drinks. He'd bet the next time the woman ordered a piña colada she'd get it. As if it mattered what he'd bet. He didn't know the bartender from the woman who delivered his laundry.

The door opened again, letting in heat, and two men wearing jeans and blue uniform shirts. Grease smeared their faces and arms. More of the dart-playing mechanics, evidently. This was the damnedest assortment of people. The only thing the different groups seemed to have in common was Cassie and not gambling.

She shook her head at the newcomers. "Really, guys? You couldn't have washed up first?" She jerked a thumb toward the back. "Go use some soap."

They grumbled, insisted they had tried to clean up, but did as she ordered.

John smiled, and for a second he caught her eye. She blinked, then looked down at the pitcher she was filling, and he polished off his beer.

"You want another?" she asked a minute later, grabbing a towel and drying her hands on her way over to him. "Or are you ready to settle up?"

"You really are trying to get rid of me."

She raised her eyebrows. Her lips parted, closed, then she said, "I wouldn't put it like that."

"Okay." He leaned back, studying her face. She was good. She didn't give anything away. "Go ahead...in your own words."

Her abrupt laugh caught him off guard. "I was trying to be considerate. This place can get rough as the evening goes on."

"So you don't think I can take care of myself?"

She ran a gaze over his shoulders, did a thorough job of checking out his chest and then lingered on his belly. Maybe even a little lower. "You'd do all right."

"Cassie," someone yelled. "These pretzels are stale."

"Well, Steve, you should've come yesterday when they weren't." She ignored the opportunity to break away and, in fact, didn't even look at the guy complaining. Or at the others who laughed. Instead she'd moved back up to John's face and stared as if she were trying to figure him out.

He slid the empty mug toward her. "You don't strike me as someone who'd let things get out of control."

"You've been here, what? All of thirty...forty minutes, and you know this about me?"

"I'm a good judge of character."

"So am I." With a faint enigmatic smile, she picked up the mug and started toward her station.

"You can use the same one," he said, noticing a slight sway to her hips.

"Oh, I planned on it." She didn't look back, just flung the words out into the universe knowing they'd hit their mark.

He chuckled, but his amusement fled when the two guys she'd sent to wash up returned and took stools at the bar. Damn it. He didn't want to share her. Not that he had a say. Already the waitress was back with more orders to fill. Cassie automatically popped open bottles of Corona and set them in front of the mechanics while she waited for the foam to settle on John's draft.

At this rate, it would be a long night. But after talking to her for those few moments, he was willing to wait around. He'd have to cool it on the drinking, but that was no problem. He knew when to quit, and sitting here beat the restlessness that had him driving too fast on the long empty desert stretches before he'd found this place.

Hearing the door open again, he gritted his teeth. She'd never have a break if this kept up. Curious who'd wandered in this time, he turned around. Another man in a wheelchair rolled in and headed toward the retired air force vet's table. The back of his chair was covered with navy decals surrounding a large American flag sticker. Following behind him was a trio who might have been cut from the same cloth, except two were lucky enough to still be upright, handicap-free, at least physically, and the third managed his severe limp with the help of a worn cane.

John assumed they were either military retirees or men who'd served their country until a bullet or spray of shrapnel changed their dreams and lives forever. These men were in their early to mid-forties with half their lives ahead of them.

His friend Danny had only been thirty when he'd died, leaving a young wife behind. They'd had no children, which was supposed to have been a "blessing." John had heard that piece of nonsense more than once at the funeral. He didn't get that. Sure, it was easier on his widow not having to explain why their father was never coming home. But kids would've meant there was still something left of Danny.

Who was John to judge? He had nothing but his career. A damn good one. He was a lucky guy. No denying it. So what the hell was his problem?

The ache in his gut was back gnawing away at his temporary peace. He hadn't even made it an hour without feeling the walls close in. When he swung back around he saw his refill sitting on the napkin in front of him. Cassie had brought his beer and he hadn't even noticed.

Watching her fill glasses with ice, he reached in his pocket and pulled out two twenties. He took a long pull of the cold brew and set the mug down on the bills. She could've been someone interesting to get to know. But she was right. This wasn't his kind of place. Certainly not his kind of people.

He got up and left, knowing he wouldn't find anywhere else more comfortable.

3

CASSIE SNAPPED HER GAZE BACK for a second look. He'd been sitting there a moment ago. His mug was almost full. Even though she didn't think he was the type to mingle, she scanned the room.

It was crowded, but no John among the other customers.

She saw that his stool had been pushed close to the bar. That was something she and Lisa did after everyone left for the night. When people went to the bathroom or stepped away, they left their stool right where it was, even if it had landed in the middle of the room.

"Lisa, did you see the flyboy leave?"

"No, but I wasn't paying attention. He didn't skip out on his tab, did he?"

Cassie leaned over the bar as far as she could to see in the back. Nothing. "What?"

"Look." Lisa pointed. "There's money under his mug."

Disappointment welled in her chest. She shouldn't care that he'd gone. She should be glad. Yes, he was hot and had a nice laugh, great eyes. But he stared too much and made her self-conscious. Still, couldn't he have finished his beer and waited for his bill? Maybe said goodbye? They'd talked a little.

She grabbed a damp rag on her way to collect the cash and wipe the bar. "Whoa," she muttered when she saw what he'd left. The tab was only seven bucks even counting the scotch. He'd left forty. She grabbed the bills and hurried out the front door.

In the crowded parking lot, she recognized half the cars, but mostly she was looking for taillights. Was she being too optimistic? She could've sworn he'd still been inside a few minutes ago.

Some customers parked on the street when only narrow stalls were left in the lot. Of course he'd come in early but she walked to the road anyway. She spotted him then, pulling away from the curb. Well, she didn't see *him* precisely, but that silver Corvette? Had to be John.

Knowing it was useless because he was too far away, she lifted a hand just in case. Because the tip was too big, and she had to at least try....

Of course, he drove off. Not that it mattered. As she hurried back to the bar she gave herself a good mental shake. Why did she give a damn that he'd given her a huge tip? Or that she'd never see him again. First of all, she didn't date, and if she did, she didn't date customers. Second, he was so far out of her league he might as well be headed for Mars.

Stopping at the door, she readjusted her ponytail, then walked back inside as she stuffed the twenties into her pocket.

Lisa stood behind the bar filling her own order. "What was that about?"

Cassie moved in to take over. "The pilot forgot his change."

"Did you catch him?"

"Nope. I was too late. Did Gordon ask for another one?" Cassie focused on filling the next order, wishing Lisa would go deliver her drinks.

"No, he's fine." She went around to the other side of the bar. "How much too much?"

"Thirty-three bucks."

Lisa let out a low whistle. "Good job. I saw you chatting him up."

She snorted. "I took him a beer. That's it."

"You were talking earlier...."

"If you say so. I don't remember." Cassie felt the heat in her cheeks and crouched to get a bowl of maraschino cherries out of the fridge. She took her time, but when she straightened, Lisa was still there.

"So...he's military, right?"

"I don't know," Cassie said, not bothering to hide her annoyance. "Would you please get these drinks out of here?"

Lisa picked up her tray. Grinning, she gave Cassie a long, amused look. "I hope he comes back."

"Don't hold your breath."

"A dollar says he does."

"You're on." Cassie kept her head down until she knew Lisa was gone.

Her friend had the wrong idea. Cassie was relieved he'd taken off. Now she didn't have to worry about Tommy noticing him and making a crack about offi-

cers. In an hour the after-work crowd would thin and
maybe she'd have a few minutes to study. If John had
stayed, her work would've remained buried under the
stack of clean rags.

Besides, she knew better than to fall for unattainable
men. That way lay madness. She had a degree to finish.
Here at the Gold Strike her world was safe and predict-
able. Being a bartender gave her what passed for a social life and put money in her pocket. It was all good.

YAWNING, JOHN FLIPPED the switch on the coffeemaker.
It was programmed to start brewing at five-thirty. That
usually worked fine…when he didn't sleep until noon.
He couldn't remember the last time he'd done that. But
then he hadn't gone to bed until nearly 4:00 a.m.

He got out a mug, then left it on the counter and
forced himself out of the kitchen. Staring at the drips
would only make him crazy while he waited for the first
cup to brew. The notebook sat on the glass coffee table
where he'd left it, open to the columns of pros and cons
he'd started around midnight.

Hell, his grocery list had been longer. He rubbed his
bare chest, then scraped the back of his knuckles along
his stubbled chin and jaw. Maybe he wouldn't shave
for ten days. Be a bum, see what it felt like not to have
to shine his boots, or to leave the condo. He had a pile
of books he'd been meaning to read, a couple issues of
AirForces Monthly to catch up on and if he wanted to
just veg out, there were enough sports channels to keep
him sprawled on the couch until it was time to make
another turkey sandwich.

Sounded okay in theory. But last night had felt like

being stuck forever in a cockpit waiting for a runway. Watching baseball on TV wasn't his thing. Going to a game was okay. If his mood hadn't gone sideways after seeing those vets, he would've stayed at the Gold Strike, eaten stale pretzels and watched the cute bartender.

With her wild chestnut hair and quick wit, he'd thought about her an awful lot. She didn't fit his image of a woman who'd work in a dive bar. Not when she could be doing so much better bartending on the Strip. The tourists would like her trivia gimmick and her attitude. But she seemed awfully comfortable in the Gold Strike. The more he thought about it, the more it seemed right that she owned the place. She acted like she was at home there. He understood that. The air force had always been home for him, which made this…whatever the hell it was, all the more frustrating.

His coffee lured him in with its seductive aroma at the same time his cell phone buzzed. He grabbed it on his way to the kitchen and when he saw it was Sam, his pace slowed. The guy was his best friend. And the last person he'd talk to about his predicament. In fact, he hadn't even told Sam he was on leave.

John thought about letting it go to voice mail, but he'd have to eventually return the call, so what was the point? Besides, Sam normally didn't call in the middle of the day. Since he couldn't fly anymore, maybe he was also having second thoughts about staying in another ten years.

Grabbing the carafe, John poured himself a cup as he answered. "Well, if it ain't Captain Sam Brody. What's up, Jaws?"

"I was expecting your voice mail," Sam said, then paused. "Where are you?"

Hell, he wasn't going to lie. "Home. I just rolled out of bed."

"Alone?"

"Uh, yeah...as far as I know."

Sam laughed. "Must've had a hell of a night. Isn't it noon there?"

"Wait." Coffee sloshed over the rim onto the counter. Cursing, John ripped off a paper towel from the roll suspended underneath the upper cabinet. "Just spilled my first cup of joe. Not a good start."

"Want to call me back later?"

"No, I'm good." He disposed of the towel and carried his cup to the living room. He stationed himself at the window and stared at the distant clear blue sky over Nellis. "What's going on?"

"I got my new orders today. They're sending me to Holloman. I'll be teaching newbies how to pilot MQ-9 Reapers."

"Now? Why didn't they wait until you re-upped?"

"What? I signed last week." Silence lapsed long enough for John to realize he'd stuck his foot in it, then Sam asked, "I gather you haven't."

"Nah, not yet. I'm on a short leave to take care of some loose ends. So how you feeling about being an instructor?"

"It's fine. It'll be good."

John had a lot of things he could have said about that, but he didn't. If Sam was cool with teaching, then he was glad for him. "When do you report?"

"I'll be taking some leave myself after I make the

move, but that won't be for about a month. I haven't actually finished my training here. You know who lives in Alamogordo, don't you?"

"Emma." John pictured Danny's widow the day of his funeral. Pale, too slender in a plain black dress, trembling, her body jerking every time a rifle fired into the air in farewell to Captain Daniel "Woody" Lockwood. "It's been three years. She might have moved by now."

"I don't think so."

"So you're going to see her?"

"I don't know. I think so, but...the last thing I want to do is open an old wound."

John sighed. "That's a tough one, buddy. She made it pretty clear she preferred to be left alone. But that might've been grief talking. If it were me, I'd at least give her a call."

"That's what I was thinking. She can always hang up on me."

"Emma wouldn't do that." John smiled. She was a nice lady, pretty, patient with Danny, who, in the pursuit of a good time, often forgot he had a wife. "But a call gives her an easy out."

"If it goes well, I'll offer to buy her dinner and do some catching up. Hey, maybe you could hop a flight sometime. See my new digs?"

"Very possible." John sipped his coffee, but still couldn't hold back a yawn.

"Man, don't you just hate when sleeping till noon wears you right out?"

John laughed. "Gee, Dad, it wasn't a school night."

"So...what do you think...you staying at Nellis?"

"I don't know." That was the truth. If he traded his uniform for civvies, the private pilot gig he was offered would keep him on the move.

"They talk to you about testing the F-35C?"

John turned away from the window and back to the kitchen. He hated even the mention of the F-35C. It was Sam who deserved to be in the cockpit, not teaching drone pilots because of his less-than-perfect eyesight.

"You there?"

"Yeah, I'm here."

"Look, Devil, I'm good with what I'm doing. No need to backpedal. Would I like to get back in the air? Damn straight I would. But that's gonna take a miracle. So quit it. You didn't make the rules."

"Yeah, yeah." John sighed, wishing he knew what to say. Wishing he knew what the hell he wanted to do for the next twenty years. "My housekeeper will be letting herself in any second, and I'm standing here in my skivvies."

Sam laughed. "Go."

"I'll call you later."

"Make it sooner."

"You got it." John disconnected the call, noticed he had a message waiting.

While he listened, he dumped the lukewarm crap and refilled his mug, making sure to drink it as he carried it into the bathroom. The voice mail was from Towlie, aka Rick, another pilot he worked with at Nellis, confirming dinner tonight, which was a good thing because John had forgotten. Two other guys were joining them on the Strip. Both from other bases who were flying in overnight. John had run into Derek a few times on assignment; the other pilot wasn't someone he knew. But he had no doubt they'd have a good time, talking shop at dinner and then club-hopping and picking up women.

Goddamn, he must be in rough shape if the thought of that sweet plan made him cringe.

IT WAS A QUIET AFTERNOON with only four customers in the bar. Mondays between noon and five at the Gold Strike were usually slow, especially toward the end of the month when people were waiting for checks.

Cassie looked up from her book to check on Gordon and his three cronies. The old guys made it easy on her. They always ordered two drinks at a time. On days like this when she worked solo and needed to study, it helped not to be constantly interrupted. That didn't mean she wouldn't wring Tommy's neck. He was supposed to have covered the afternoon shift. But he'd claimed he had bar business to take care of. Bar business, her butt.

He barely wrote or signed checks anymore, or verified invoices or shopped for the garnishes. No, he just dumped everything on her lap. And like a fool, she let him.

Gordon caught her glaring at the door. "Your folks still in Oregon, Cassie?"

"Yep. They're likely to stay till fall."

"Can't blame 'em. This whole valley feels like a damn oven. Hotter than last summer and no one can tell me otherwise."

Cassie agreed. She'd just paid last month's electric bill, and wow, had that stung. She'd had to cut into what she jokingly referred to as her salary to cover costs, and tips weren't always that great. Last night's thirty-three dollars had been awesome. She hoped John came back. But only because he was such a good tipper. "You guys want pretzels?"

"Nah, we might order a pepperoni pizza," Gordon said. "You interested?"

She glanced at the clock...already three-thirty. "I'll pass. As soon as Tommy gets here, I'm shoving off."

"You need me to watch the bar?"

Sighing, Cassie shook her head. "Thanks, but I don't know what time he'll be here." If he didn't show up within two hours, she was screwed. Lisa started at five, but she couldn't handle the after-work crowd by herself, so Cassie would have no choice but to stay.

Gordon gave her his famous raised eyebrow. Which was saying something, because his brows were bushy, pure white and as expressive as a cartoon character's. "What's he gonna do without you?"

"Why? Where am I going?"

"Once you get that master's degree, you won't be sticking around. You've got too many brains to be working here as it is."

"I don't know about that." She pushed her fingers through her tangled hair. "Besides, who'd keep you guys in line?"

Gordon frowned. "Nobody's gotta worry about me. My hell-raising days are over."

Joe muttered something about Gordon being too slow to get into trouble. The other old boys hooted with laughter and added their two cents.

Cassie just smiled. All four were retired military, ornery and gruff when they played poker or argued over the superiority of the air force versus the navy. But they were harmless, and ready to step in and help her out when she was in a bind.

"Shut up," Gordon said. "Let the girl study in peace." He tossed a take-out menu across the table. "Are we ordering pizza or not?"

She took another look at the clock, knowing only two minutes had passed, and then stared down at her textbook. Studying psychology wasn't a hardship. She loved observing people and discovering what made them tick. But it was this extra class on neurorehabilitation that was going to kill her. She'd passed cognitive neuroscience with relative ease, but this one was surprisingly more difficult for her. Maybe because she hadn't had nearly enough sleep and too little study time.

But she wouldn't beat herself up for being too ambitious. Her only fault had been overestimating Tommy. He knew she'd chosen an aggressive summer schedule, assured her that he was behind her all the way, and then he'd let her down. Was it intentional?

She doubted it. He was a good man at heart, but stubborn. And since he wouldn't go for counseling, she was left to struggle with his decisions. It wouldn't be so bad if those decisions didn't impact her so acutely. On the other hand, he wasn't actively trying to harm himself anymore, so that was something.

Their parents wouldn't be here to help him out. They hadn't believed in him enlisting, much less fighting a war in Iraq and getting his leg blown off. Neither of them were monsters, but they weren't vying for a parents-of-the-year award, either. They had their own lives, and Cassie appreciated that they didn't interfere in hers.

The room was quiet enough that she heard a car engine outside. Probably Tommy's van, which he parked at a reserved spot near the handicap ramp. She stared at the door, and two minutes later, watched him limp over the threshold.

He met her eyes for a second, then swung his gaze toward Gordon and the gang. "Joe, you gotta move your car. It's taking up two stalls."

"I did that on purpose," Joe said, looking up from the menu, his gray-threaded dark hair hanging limply to his shoulders. "I'm saving a space for Spider's Harley." He pulled out his cell phone. "I'm calling in a couple pizzas. You eat yet?"

Tommy waved him off and kept walking toward Cassie. "I told you we should be serving food here," he murmured when he passed close enough for her alone to hear.

"Right. Because I don't have enough responsibility to juggle as it is." Her blood pressure skyrocketed when she realized he was headed for the back. "Don't you dare—"

He stopped, slowly turned. "What?"

"You don't think you might owe me just the tiniest explanation why you're late?"

"Can I at least take a piss first?"

"No, you can't." She gritted her teeth when the others laughed. She hadn't meant for them to hear. "Where the hell were you?"

"I told you I had bar business."

Boy, had he just opened himself up. She bit back the sarcastic remark that came to mind. "Such as?"

"I don't wanna talk to you about it when you're in

this kind of mood. You'll just be negative and give me attitude." He continued on to the back room.

She slipped around and followed him. "You knew I had to study, and you promised you'd cover this afternoon. Now you're gonna explain what was so damn important that you screwed me over."

Tommy sighed and turned to meet her gaze. He was clean shaven, not a regular occurrence, and he'd tamed his curly hair. "Can you keep an open mind?"

She glanced at his wrinkle-free shirt, a button-down, not his usual ragged T-shirt. Maybe he was telling her the truth. "Yes, I can."

"I met with the attorney about the gaming commission. If things go well with the background checks, we could have the license by November."

"Are you kidding me?" Had he not listened to a word she'd said? The Gold Strike was in no position to consider gaming.

"See, there you go with the attitude."

"I thought you were joking about this. Even if you could get the license you can't afford to pay someone to keep the place open twenty-four hours."

"Do you know how much money those machines pull in? We'll be able to hire three more people if we want. Put in a kitchen and serve food instead of watching customers bring in pizzas and hot wings. This place could be so much better."

"Look…it's not—" Cassie got a false start, breathed in deeply and tried again. She didn't want to crush his enthusiasm, just inject a dose of reality. "I'm not against making improvements or expanding. It simply won't happen in the near future. Tommy, the license is a half-million dollars."

He shrugged and his face flushed. "Len has some ideas about that."

"What kind of ideas?" She moved closer. "You didn't have enough in the account to cover the electric bill. I had to dig into my own pocket."

"Why didn't you tell me?"

She stared at him in mute frustration, waiting for him to remember that she had told him. But his personal coffers had also been bare.

Shame burning in his hazel eyes, he looked away. "We can find a way to make it work. We just have to be creative."

Cassie didn't bother to argue, or to point out there would be no "we." Sad for both of them, she watched him walk toward the men's room, his shoulders slumped. He scared her when he got like this.

Whoever this attorney was, he was outright stealing from Tommy if he was telling him they were in any position to get a license. At least now she knew why Tommy never had a nickel in the bank. The right thing to do would be to track this shyster down and file a complaint against him. Which might save the bar, but could destroy her brother.

Maybe he needed to hit bottom before he'd start living in the real world again. But she wasn't strong enough to watch him fall.

4

AFTER SUFFERING THROUGH bumper-to-bumper traffic for three blocks, John finally turned on Flamingo. Another minute and he merged onto I-15, glad to be away from the Strip and the tourists. He hadn't minded leaving Rick and the other two men behind, either.

Dinner with the guys was supposed to have boosted his spirits, remind him of the camaraderie he enjoyed in the air force. Not depress him. Halfway through the meal he knew he wouldn't be joining them afterward at the Palms for drinks and hunting. Maybe he shouldn't have left so early. A beautiful woman in his bed might be just the distraction he needed. On the other hand, the mood he was in, he doubted he'd want anyone that close.

It was Troy, the pilot he hadn't met before, who'd sent John into a funk. In the middle of their discussion about the F-35, he'd gotten a call from his wife. She'd put their two kids on the phone so he could say good-night to them, then Troy told her he loved her and missed her. Seconds after Troy disconnected he asked Rick where they were going clubbing.

No one at the table had batted an eye. Not even John.

None of his business, and it wasn't as if he didn't know that kind of crap went on all the time, but Jesus, the guy had just talked to his wife and kids. How did a man run cold to hot that fast after telling a woman he loved her?

Granted, John wasn't an expert on love or marriage. Twice he'd thought he'd been in love, once in college and then again five years ago. Both ended up being false alarms. Greta and Tricia each had been fun, sexy, amazing women in their own way, just not right for him. But while they'd been together, he'd never cheated on either of them, never considered it for a minute.

He sped past the exit for his condo. He hadn't planned on going to the Gold Strike, so it wasn't the reason he'd bailed. But he didn't want to go home, either. It was early, only nine. And he wouldn't mind seeing Cassie again.

Thinking about the cute bartender made him smile. He'd be disappointed as hell if she wasn't working tonight, but he doubted she took much time off. The bar was her domain and the customers her family. Everyone seemed to get a real kick out of trying to stump her with trivia. They put some thought into the questions he'd heard, but no matter how busy she'd been, Cassie had known the answer. He'd never seen anything like it. Like her.

Traffic thinned the farther he got away from the Strip and downtown, and it didn't take long to get to the Gold Strike. The parking lot was less crowded than last night but he looked for a spot on the street anyway. Maybe he was wrong in thinking the Corvette was safer at the curb, but the stalls were narrow and he'd watched more than a few guys putting away too many pitchers of beer.

At one point early last night Cassie had cut off a burly man with bikers' tats. John had moved to the edge of his stool ready to intervene, then saw she hadn't needed help. The guy hadn't given her any grief. Another man with arms the size of oak trees and wearing lots of biker leather had emerged from the back room. No doubt he would've bounced the drunk all the way to the California state line if he'd uttered one wrong word to Cassie.

John parked the Corvette and pocketed his keys on the way to the door. If he'd thought about it earlier, he would've changed into jeans. Though he wouldn't stand out too much in dark slacks and a white oxford shirt, not in that eclectic crowd. In deference to the heat, he rolled his sleeves back another turn and, all right, he hoped he didn't look too preppy.

As soon as he stepped inside he saw her behind the bar, sitting with her head bowed. Over a book. A couple sat a few stools down from her, both with full cocktails in front of them. His seat from last night was free, and he pulled it away from the bar. Lisa, the waitress, came from the back room and smiled at him. She set her tray near Cassie and said something, probably alerting her that she had a customer, because Cassie's chin came up and she looked right at him.

Quick as a wink, she shoved her book under a pile of towels, then took out a frosted mug and filled it with beer. Once again, she'd worn tight faded jeans and a T-shirt, black this time, and not so snug, which was a shame. When she carried the drink over to him, he saw an outline of a cat on the front of her shirt.

His gaze switched to the beer she put in front of him. "How do you know this is what I want?"

"I'd be happy to pour you a scotch."

He smiled and picked up the mug. "I guess this makes me a regular."

"Nope. Come in five days a week for six months and then maybe...."

"That's some serious drinking. I don't know...I could embarrass myself."

She finally smiled. "A tab, or do you want to pay up in case you have another emergency?"

It took him a moment. "Ah, last night, right." He took a sip. "I forgot I had to be somewhere."

"That reminds me..." She reached into her back pocket, pulling the stretchy T-shirt across her breasts.

He stared at the cat, saw that it wasn't just a cat. There was an equation written out within the outline.

"Are you trying to figure out what the cat represents or my cup size?"

John huffed out a short laugh. He'd have to remember she didn't pull punches. "I was just admiring Mr. Schrödinger's cat. I've never seen it expressed quite so well."

She tried not to smile as she pulled out some bills and laid them on the bar. "It'll be the last time I wear the shirt in here, because trying to explain it to these lunkheads all day has given me a headache."

"What's that for?" he asked, when she slid the money closer to him.

"Your change from last night. You left before I could cash you out."

"That's your tip."

"Thirty-three dollars?"

He shrugged.

Cassie pursed her lips. She had a nice mouth. "Are you sure? I bet you didn't think you were leaving that much."

"I'm sure."

"All right." She snatched the bills and stuffed them into her front pocket. "What do you do for a living? Can't have anything to do with finance."

He smiled, his mood already improved. "No, but you don't have to explain T-shirts to me, either."

She gave him that one with a nod and a grin, but then Lisa called for her to fill an order and Cassie snapped back to her duties. Tugging at her ponytail, she returned to her station. It gave him a chance to admire her cute, slightly upturned nose and the long graceful curve of her neck. He already knew she had a nice behind but he was careful not to ogle.

He hoped she came back to talk to him after she finished. The couple sitting closer to her were nursing their drinks, so they didn't need anything. He turned to check out the tables. The older guys in the corner were okay for now. They had a number of beers and shots waiting. John recognized the group from last night, even before spotting the retired air force ball cap, and he nodded to the vet in the wheelchair who stared at him.

The man didn't acknowledge the overture, but that was okay. Maybe he was protective of Cassie and didn't like her talking to the new guy. Maybe he'd even pegged John as military or, worse, an officer. He'd run across his share of sergeants who lived to serve their country, honored rank but had no use for the men wearing the stripes. Unfortunately, he also knew a number of officers who didn't deserve respect.

In that regard the military was like any other business, he supposed. The people at the top weren't always the brightest and the best. Right now he only cared that Cassie didn't know he was air force. Or that he was a pilot. To someone like her it probably didn't matter. Still, for once he just wanted to be John, a guy drinking a beer and talking to the bartender.

Within five minutes the pool players ordered half a dozen pitchers and more customers spilled into the bar. John clenched his jaw each time the door opened, not sure if he was upset because she was kept away from her studies or from talking to him. She was efficient, and he'd done worse things than watch her move, but at this rate, he'd have to empty his mug to get her attention again. He shouldn't resent it. More customers meant more tips for her.

Hell, he'd just wait everyone out. He wasn't tired, and didn't expect he would be for a while. He lifted his mug, but set it aside before he drank. He liked beer just fine, as long as it was cold. She'd see it and know that he wanted another one. When she looked over at him, he mouthed for her not to rush.

His phone buzzed, signaling a text. Even before he looked he knew it had to be Rick.

It was a simple message: · · · — — — · · ·

John hadn't expected the SOS. He laughed, imagining the scene at the Palms. It seemed his dinner companions had hit the mother lode. And now they had more women than they could handle.

He hit Text. You're on your own.

While he waited to see if there was a response, someone sat at the bar a couple stools away from him. He briefly glanced over and saw it was actually two women, young, maybe college age. Standing behind them was a third woman with long blond hair that hid most of her face.

"Hey, Cassie." The brunette with the really short hair, who was sitting, waited for Cassie to look at her then signaled that there were three of them. "When you have a chance."

John caught Cassie's nod before he checked Rick's return text. It turned out to be a picture of a redhead. She had a lot of makeup and wore a low-cut top that left nothing to his imagination. He hadn't been a kid who peeked at his presents before Christmas morning. When he unwrapped a package, he preferred to be surprised.

Thanks, but I'll pass.

Once he hit Send, he turned off his phone and slipped it into his pocket as Cassie approached, carrying three mugs. "What are you guys doing here on a Tuesday?" she asked the women while setting down their beers.

"We've got one for you."

John felt a shift in the atmosphere. Those sitting at the bar all turned to look at the girls, and it wasn't because they were pretty.

CASSIE SIGHED AS KARMA reached between her friends for her mug. "I want a shot with this. Shall I get it myself?"

"I'll get it." Cassie looked at Ariel, who'd spent a little too much time at the tanning booth. "Who's driving?"

"Brittney," she said as she tilted her head at her pale friend sitting beside her. "I'll have a shot with Karma."

"Wait," Brittney said. "I don't think it's my turn."

The other two laughed. "That's because you were too drunk to remember that I drove last week," Karma said.

Cassie took a deep breath and turned her attention to John. She picked up his beer mug, gave him a smile, then walked back to her station, hoping whatever the terrible trio had in mind would be harmless.

Pouring a shot of tequila, she noticed Karma noticing John. Her double take was like something out of a movie. Not that Cassie could argue with that—she'd had the same reaction. A couple of nudges later, and all three of them were staring at him with about as much subtlety as a two-ton truck. Cassie should do something about it, although she figured he could take care of himself. Besides, she was curious about his reaction to the girls. They were all legal, of course, but they were young and hot and she wasn't sure if John was a player or not.

He had to know they were staring at him as if they'd discovered Johnny Depp had wandered into the bar. Damn. What would they be like after they had their shots?

Cassie walked back with John's beer, and only John's beer. She stood right in front of him. After she put down the mug she planted her hands on the bar in a very territorial display. "You doing okay?"

He gave the girls the side-eye, then smiled. "Just fine."

"Good. Enjoy the rest of the game."

It took him a few beats too long to look up at the TV.

She had no idea what game it was, but it didn't matter. He now had a reason to ignore the women, and they had a reason to leave him the hell alone.

She'd have done the same for anyone.

She sidled over to the girls. "What's this big stumper of yours?"

"It's a killer," Ariel said.

"Hush up," Karma said. "It's my question."

"Karma. Stop. I don't have time for this. I don't care whose question it is, you'd better ask it or I'm not playing."

"Oh, you'll want to play," the blonde replied, flipping her hair back behind her shoulder.

"Why is that?"

"Because you're never gonna get it."

"What's the subject?"

"TV."

She went back to her station and picked up the two shots for the girls, wondering how long it would take for people to buy a clue. Every time she was challenged it was with absolute certainty that their question was so obscure she'd never get it in a million years. Cassie just shook her head. "I wouldn't be so sure."

The three girls laughed, then Ariel and Karma threw back their drinks.

"The question is," Cassie said, "what do I win when I get it in less than sixty seconds?"

The noise level from the rest of the bar had gone down considerably. Which always happened when someone challenged her reign as trivia queen. It was getting kind of old, but she couldn't complain. Everyone bought rounds after she answered, either cussing her out or congratulating themselves. The gimmick was good for business.

"Winner's choice," Ariel said, just before she slammed her empty shot glass down on the bar.

That quieted the whole damn place...well, at least the main room. Cassie could still hear the pool players going at it. "You're crazy if you think I'm doing that. Look, I've got to study, and Lisa's up to her eyeballs in orders, so, tell you what, let's not play and say we did."

She saw John's surprised reaction, which gave her a twinge of guilt for being so curt. "I'm sorry," she said, sort of sincerely. "I honestly don't have time." She turned away with a shrug and hoped they'd let it go.

"But that's exactly why you should play," Karma said, grinning. "Because if you win, your choice could be us taking over behind the bar for a couple of hours."

Cassie stopped. Turned. But instead of facing off with Karma, her gaze went to John. He'd clearly given up all pretense of watching anything but the little drama unfolding right next to him. Cassie should shut it down, tell them to wait for another time, but she had to admit it was tempting. Acing her test was beginning to feel like an impossible dream. Now she faced her challenger. "You tend bar? *Please.* You barely know how to drink, let alone mix."

Karma, who really did have a big mouth, just raised an insouciant eyebrow. "How hard can it be? Pour a beer, wash a mug, pour another beer."

"Oh, yeah? I win, you take the bar for two hours. Then we'll see how easy it is, Princess."

"What if I win?" Karma asked.

"You won't."

"Still."

Cassie narrowed her eyes. "Winner's choice."

A chorus of "Ohhhhhhh" came from the spectators. Cassie didn't give a spit about anyone out there, she just wanted to win. Well, almost anyone. John had not only forgotten the TV, he hadn't taken a sip of his beer yet. Odd, his gaze stayed directly on her. Even with Karma's provocative statements, he hadn't given the blonde so much as a glance.

"Deal." Karma lifted up her beer mug. "Let the record show the game is on."

Cassie's eye roll should have gotten applause, but everyone was too caught up in the ridiculous game. "I haven't got all night."

"Okay, Cassie O'Brien. For the championship. What is Spencer Reid's IQ?"

Cassie let out a breath. Of course she knew that. It was *Criminal Minds*. She was a huge fan of the TV show, and especially Spencer. Or Hotch.

It was 187. Or was it 189? Damn. Her first instinct was right. It was always right. She opened her mouth to say the number then remembered the quiz she'd had in her class last week. She'd gone with her first instinct and she'd been wrong.

"Tick tock," Ariel said, her voice far too jovial.

"I have the right to refuse service to anyone," Cassie said. "So keep it zipped." She had to choose. She'd go with her first guess, because that was a deeper memory, one that came from the source.

"Time!" Ariel jumped up from her bar stool, flinging beer like confetti as she raised her glass to Karma. "You won! You won! You rock so hard!"

Cassie couldn't breathe. How had...? No way had she lost to Karma and her college cronies. No possible way. There was a mistake. A drunk girl had kept time, it couldn't be right. She'd had the answer on the tip of her tongue.

The noise was worse than midnight on New Year's Eve. Seriously. Everyone was shouting. Even the old goats were banging on tables. Gordon was twirling his wheelchair, and that man could barely lift a glass.

It was only a game. And only her first loss. Her face shouldn't be blazing hot. The only thing to do was be gracious as all hell. Smile like she meant it. Give the girls their due.

She'd have plenty of time later to poison their drinks.

THE BAR HAD GONE BERSERK around John, but all he could do was stare. Not at the mayhem, but at Cassie. He'd had no idea this competition of hers was so fierce. More than the reaction from the patrons, watching her face had told him just how deep the cut of losing went. But he had to give it to her. She was rallying like a champion. From the straightening of her shoulders to the almost real smile on her face, she looked as though she'd stumbled, not fallen. Somehow, she'd even managed to tame her blush. Very impressive.

He still felt terrible for her. If he could have, he'd have swept her out of here, taken her somewhere far removed, like up to Mount Charleston to look out over the valley.

As it was, he did his best not to look pitying. Although she hadn't glanced at him since time had run out.

Karma was the one to actually calm the crowd down.

Not completely, but for a bunch of people fueled by alcohol, she did a damn good job. Her ear-piercing whistle helped. "Quiet. It's winner's choice time."

Another round of stomping and shouting took several minutes to run its course, but then all eyes were whipping between Karma and Cassie.

John was all ears himself. He hoped there wouldn't be anything too humiliating involved because if that happened, he might have to step in. It wasn't his place, but he didn't care.

"All right, what do I have to do?" Cassie said.

"First, you can bring me and my friends a round."

"If that's your request, then that's going to be it. Nothing in the rules says you get a laundry list."

Karma pouted extravagantly. "Fine. But see if you get a tip."

"I'll live," Cassie said, her arms crossing her chest. She looked like a little spitfire. Which was something John would never say out loud for fear of being clocked. But he'd think it.

"What you have to do, Cassie, is kiss..." Karma turned around and faced the center of the room. A hush gave the moment all the drama of the last pitch of a no-hitter. Karma's gaze settled on a moose of a man, bigger than a redwood tree trunk and painted with more ink than the Mona Lisa. The old bear's grin showed exactly how many teeth he'd lost to time.

Then Karma spun around, pointed a long, red nail directly at John, and said, "That guy."

5

JOHN STOPPED. Breathing, blinking, thinking. All he could see was a pointing finger, and the rest of his vision had gone white. As if he'd been disconnected, like an unplugged TV set. It only lasted a few seconds, but when he came back on line, the world seemed to gear up in jerks and starts until he felt truly back in the Gold Strike bar, somehow landing in the middle of a game he hadn't been playing.

"Karma," Cassie said, her voice about a half octave higher than it had been. "Don't be ridiculous. Come on, I need to get back to work."

"Oh, no," Karma said, literally licking her lips with pleasure. "I'm the winner. You lost. It's my choice."

"Not when it involves a stranger," Cassie said. "Pick something else."

"There's nothing in the rules that says it can't be a stranger." She looked around the bar. "Is there?"

The chorus chimed in, egging her on, of course.

John's gaze went to Cassie, though. The embarrassed flush he expected, because he was pretty warm himself, but he needed to see more, to see if she was seri-

ous about putting her foot down or just trying to give
him an out.

He didn't know her well enough to be sure, but he'd
gotten a vibe from her last night and tonight that a kiss
wouldn't offend her. He'd been planning on trying just
that after the bar closed. The last thing he wanted was
for this stunt to take away any chance at all.

She couldn't meet his eyes. Not for long, anyway.
She kept looking, then ducking, then looking again.
Probably trying to figure out his reaction.

He smiled. Making sure it wasn't in any possible
way lascivious or greedy or slick. Just reassuring. Letting her know that he'd gladly play along, and that he
wouldn't make a big deal out of it.

Her blush deepened after her next peek but he had
no clue what that meant.

"You wouldn't mind, would you?" Karma asked,
suddenly standing closer to him.

"Only if the lady is willing and would find it amus-
ing."

"Now, see?" Karma said, turning to Cassie. "He's
being a good sport. And a real gentleman." She looked
at him again and tilted her head. "Maybe I should save
you the trouble, Cassie, and take this one for the team."

"You step away from him right now," Cassie said.
"I'm not joking."

Not only did Karma grin, but a whole bunch of the
crowd also laughed. Was it the seriousness of Cassie's
tone? Or the idea that she was trying to protect his
honor?

"What's your name, gorgeous?" Karma had clearly

dismissed Cassie's warning. "And how come you haven't been in here before?"

John wasn't sure how to play this. He'd been stuck in awkward situations before, mostly courtesy of other pilots who were basically twelve when it came to punking, but never when someone else was the fall guy. "Name's John and I have been here before. More important, I've been around long enough to know that our friend here is trying to do her job, and we're not letting her. So if it's all the same to you, I'll make things easy on her and take my leave."

The crowd didn't like that answer, but he didn't give a crap about the crowd. He wanted to make things better for Cassie. That was all. Well, not all. It couldn't hurt his chances if he went for gallant at this stage of the proceedings.

"Oh, for God's sake," Cassie said, walking around to the patron's side of the bar. "Thank you, John, for being a real gentleman. I appreciate the gesture. And you're right, I do need to get to work. So rather than keep up this ridiculous farce, I'd be grateful if you'd let me kiss you. It won't take a second."

"It has to be on the mouth, you know," Karma said.

"Bull," Cassie replied, never moving her gaze from his.

"I don't mind," he said, lowering his voice so the whole place didn't hear. He stood, moved in close enough to see the gold flecks in her hazel eyes. "If you wanted to make a point, I would have no objections."

"What point would that be?"

He leaned down until his lips brushed against the

shell of her ear. "That you came out the winner after all?"

She huffed out a breath, but as he straightened, her hand cupped the nape of his neck to hold him steady as she pushed up into a kiss that was went from zero to Mach 2 in three seconds.

He wrapped his arms around her as she held him in place and it was all he could do to let her stay in control when he wanted to sweep in like a perfect Lothario and steal her breath with his mad skills.

It came as a very welcome surprise when the tip of her tongue swept across the seam of his lips. He parted them and she slipped inside, and if this was how she wanted to play it, he would give it his best shot.

The catcalls faded behind the sound of his own blood coursing through his veins, the increase in his heartbeat providing a rhythm that somehow she must have felt, because they were completely in sync. The parry and thrust, the quick stolen breaths, the way she moved in the same moment he pulled her close.

His hand spread on her back as the taste of her won out over his last sip of beer. Thank God, because she was amazing. Coffee and mint, as if she'd mixed it herself, a perfect concoction made specifically to tempt him.

He felt a small vibration, as if she'd moaned or whimpered, he couldn't tell which, but whatever it was, it was a good thing, and if he had his way, the next time that happened he would wring out all her sounds for his ears only.

When she pulled back, he pressed harder, not willing to stop, but then he remembered who she was and that this was her stage and he was just a bit player.

He let her go slowly, adjusting to lights that felt too harsh, noise that made him wince.

Before she let the back of his neck go, she murmured, "Thank you."

"My pleasure."

She smiled, then turned to face her nemesis. John hoped Cassie got as much satisfaction seeing the look on Karma's face, complete with dropped jaw, as he did. He'd consider it a resounding success, but only if it was the first kiss of many.

CASSIE NEEDED A MINUTE. Or thirty. That was not what she'd planned on doing. It was supposed to have *appeared* like a major kiss, given the impression of passion and lust, that was all. Instead, her brain had gone fuzzy as everything but *oh, God, yes* had taken over. *More* had been in there, too. She couldn't forget *more*.

She wouldn't forget him.

Karma's defeat helped bring her back to her senses, because it was too good to miss. The brazen blonde looked utterly shocked. Her eyes wide, her cheeks flushed, her mouth open. It was awesome. If only she'd had her cell phone with her, she'd have captured the moment for posterity. "Are we done now?" Cassie asked in her most impatient tone.

Karma closed her mouth and sniffed. "I still won," she said.

"Sure you did, kid," Cassie said, then headed back to the sink behind the bar, where she proceeded to wash out the mugs that had accumulated in her absence.

Behind her, Lisa bent low and whispered, "You're my hero. That was legendary."

Cassie allowed herself a smirk. When she looked up again, Karma and her friends were on their way out, Ariel stealing one last glance at John before the door blocked her view.

Cassie stole a glimpse herself. John was back on his stool, sipping his beer, calm and cool and more handsome than seemed fair. He met her gaze as if she'd called his name, his slow grin part simmer, part promise.

Which was a problem. A much, much bigger problem than it had been half an hour ago. She didn't date customers. She didn't date airmen. She most certainly didn't date pilots. But that kiss...

That kiss had knocked her for a loop. He'd made her knees weak and her heart flutter. She'd been attracted, sure. She had eyes, and he'd impressed her with his behavior in a very awkward situation. But the kiss. Damn. She hadn't thought that through.

It had been a long time since she'd been kissed. And she'd never been kissed like *that*.

THIRTY MINUTES LATER, and John still couldn't think of anything but Cassie and that kiss. Her hair was longer than he'd thought. The jerking motion of her arm as she washed the bar top had loosened her ponytail, allowing relaxed curls to trail her neck and skim her jiggling breasts. He tried damn hard not to stare. Jesus, she had to stop scrubbing sometime. Or at least look at him. If he'd blown it with her... They barely knew each other. He could have gotten a lot more with a lot less trouble if he'd gone to the Palms with the guys. Somehow, though, he had the feeling Cassie would be worth it.

"Hey, beautiful." A guy he vaguely recognized from last night had come from the back room and headed straight for Cassie.

She looked up with a smile John was beginning to recognize. This one said, *I'm nice, but watch yourself,* whereas some of the customers got genuine warmth. "What can I do for you?"

The kid reached across the bar for a cocktail napkin, then made eyes at her. "Run away with me."

"Let me know when you're out of short pants and I'll think about it." She tossed aside the rag. "Beer? Pretzels? What?"

"I'm your age, sweetheart," he said, straightening, and looking annoyed. "When are you gonna start taking me seriously?"

"Oh, I don't know…maybe when you start acting your age." She sighed. "What can I get for you?"

John hid his smile behind a sip. She was fierce, this one.

Shaking his head, the guy used the napkin to wipe pool chalk off his fingers. "A Miller. It's for Tommy."

Cassie's features tightened. "He can't wait for Lisa, or come get it himself?"

"Don't put me in the middle."

"Tommy did that," she murmured under her breath, but John heard it. She went for the beer then set the bottle on the bar. "What about you?"

"I'm working on a pitcher. Your dishwasher still out?"

"Yep, so no, you're not getting a clean mug."

Chuckling, he grabbed the bottle and as he moved toward the back room said over his shoulder, "Think about what I said...one word and I'll take you away from all this."

"Are you kidding?" Cassie spread a hand. "And leave my world of glamour and thrills?" A smile tugged at her lips but didn't make it full-term. "Hey, Steve—"

He stopped at the door to the back room.

"Remind Tommy he's supposed to cover for me soon, would you?"

Steve nodded. "Sure."

Before he turned away, a booming voice from the main room said, "Cassie doesn't date customers, buddy."

With a dismissive flap of his hand, Steve disappeared from sight.

It was the wheelchair-bound vet in the corner who'd made the general announcement, and considering the death glare heading his way John was real clear the message was meant for him, not Steve. That kiss hadn't just shocked Karma.

He didn't mind. Good for Cassie having protective people around her. But John was more interested in Cassie's plans for later on. Was she leaving? Did she have a date? Was that why she needed someone to cover for her?

She took care of a couple drink orders and then made her way back to him. "Did you want pretzels?" she asked, as if he were just another customer.

"No, thanks. I'll pass."

"I just opened a new bag." Smiling, she leaned back on her elbows, facing him, her T-shirt stretching across her breasts.

He focused on her face, using her chin as his boundary. Anything below was off-limits. No looking, even though he could make a case for studying Schrödinger's cat. But that would make it too easy to lose himself in the memory of how soft she'd felt against him. "The older man in the wheelchair…"

"Gordon?"

"I don't know…the one who said you don't date customers."

Cassie blinked, then looked past John. "Yep, that was Gordon."

"Is it true?"

She pulled her elbows off the back counter and stood straighter. "Absolutely, one hundred percent true."

"Ah." He'd already figured as much. "Because you own the place?"

"I don't. My brother does." She leaned over the bar to see into the back room. "Not that you'd know it. He's playing darts with his friends instead of working up here like he's supposed to."

He glanced down at the view of her backside, but quickly raised his gaze before he was caught. "Why won't you date customers?"

"For one thing, I'm too busy. And secondly, eww."

He frowned. "I'm not real clear on that last point."

"Everybody practically knows everybody in here, and if things went south and it got messy…" She rolled her eyes as if she couldn't bear to think about that for another second. "People would choose sides, and who needs that aggravation?"

John had to laugh. She was probably right. "So dating a regular is the problem, not someone who's only shown up a couple times."

Her gaze narrowed. "What are you trying to say?"

"Hypothetically, if I were to ask you out, would I get shot down?"

She seemed startled, but he'd surprised himself, as well. He'd never been one to test the water before jumping in. He'd been lucky when it came to women. But he couldn't read Cassie. He had a feeling his luck might have run out.

"Hypothetically, huh?" Her lips started to curve, but then something caught her eye, because she turned abruptly toward the back.

Without a word she moved to the other end of the bar, where she filled orders. A guy with a limp was coming from the back room and met her there. *Her brother?* Yeah, John could see some resemblance despite the man's scowl. Cassie wasn't looking too happy herself.

They talked for a minute, voices low, her shooting annoyed looks at the clock behind the bar. When Lisa moved in to unload empty glasses off her tray, the man left to talk to the guys sitting in the corner. He didn't seem eager to take over for Cassie, and selfishly, John hoped she stayed behind the bar for a while longer.

As soon as Lisa hefted her tray of fresh drinks, Cassie walked over with a slip of paper in her hand. John knew it was his tab, and that she was leaving. Damn it. Obviously she had someplace to go. He wouldn't hold her up.

"You can pay up now," she said, her eyes level with his, as if trying to communicate something she hesitated to say outright. "But you don't have to. I'm leaving for the night. If Tommy ignores you, Lisa will bring you refills."

Her brother was laughing with Gordon's group. "Why would he ignore me?"

"Tommy's—" Sighing, she shook her head. "Well, he's not a total ass, but he can be moody." With a resigned expression, she met John's eyes, opened her mouth to say something else, but reconsidered. Her gaze drifted toward Tommy, and she laid down the slip of paper.

John dug out his wallet.

"Really, you don't have to settle up this minute."

"I'm heading out, too." He peeled off two tens. "Sitting here won't be much fun without you."

"Right. Because I've been a barrel of laughs." She stared down at the money he set in front of her. "I'll be back with your change."

"Nope. Keep it."

"You're horrible at math, you know that?"

John ignored the disapproval in her voice and slipped his wallet into his back pocket. His military ID had been in plain view until he remembered and did a quick shuffle. He hoped she hadn't seen it. Probably not. She seemed preoccupied. He glanced down at his tab again and noticed some writing on the bottom. Her full name. An address. A time. And the word *tomorrow* with a question mark.

He looked up at her.

She was blushing again, not nearly as much as she had when she'd lost. But she also was looking at him with serious eyes. "This is not a date," she said. "Let me repeat. Not. A. Date. But it is dinner. As a thank-you. You were great tonight, and I appreciate it."

He felt as though he'd won something big. First the kiss, and now this? "Tomorrow is good. I'll be there."

"Cassie," Tommy yelled across the room. "Two more gin and tonics."

Her gaze became a glare. "I will remain calm," she muttered. "I will not strangle him. At least not in front of witnesses."

"If I had a nickel for every time my sister said that about me…"

"You mean, you're not perfect?"

"Not by a mile." He stood, shoved his stool under the lip of the bar. He wanted to get the hell out of there before she could change her mind. She might not call it a date, but that didn't mean it couldn't be the start of something great.

She headed for the gin bottle. He hurried to the door. One last look behind him found her watching him leave. He nodded. She ducked her head and poured.

6

TRAFFIC WAS BAD and normally John wouldn't have suffered the bottleneck so graciously, but he was early to pick up Cassie, so he could afford to be patient. He'd mapped out her address and had a good idea where he was going. If he had to wait in the car until six-thirty, so be it.

Cassie O'Brien. He thought back to his college days, to the women he'd dated or more recent hookups, whether arranged by friends' wives or after a night of club-hopping, and he couldn't think of anyone like her. Not even close. She was unique, all right, and refreshing. She spoke her mind, wasn't obsessed about her appearance and yet, every time he looked at her, he liked what he saw. A lot.

He turned down her street, surprised to see a lineup of apartment buildings. Her address was in his top pocket and he pulled it out for another look. She hadn't given him a unit number. Damn. Had she done that on purpose? No, that made no sense. He knew where she worked.

Slowing to a crawl, he systematically checked each

building address. When he got to the end of the street he saw a trio of duplexes, all painted tan but each with its own number. The first one on the left was Cassie's. There was a Ford four-door parked in the driveway. The car had to be over fifteen years old and looked like something Stephen King might use for a character.

He parked at the curb with eight minutes to spare. With the air-conditioning on he listened to an old Van Morrison CD while he checked out her neighborhood. Very blue-collar, clean, neat, with obvious pride taken in the small lawns and flower beds. Cassie's grass had recently been mowed and a large pot of yellow and pink flowers sat on the porch.

At six twenty-eight he knocked on the front door. It needed a fresh coat of paint. He saw a curtain move and then heard the doorknob turn.

"Hey," she said, swinging the door open and stepping back. Her hair was down, bouncing in loose curls around her shoulders. "Come in."

"Hi." He stared at her shorts, jeans that had been chopped off, leaving the hem frayed. Man, she had a great pair of legs.

"The place is kind of a mess. I didn't have a chance to organize the chaos by the time I got home," she said, gesturing him to the left. "But the kitchen is okay."

"You just got home?"

"About an hour ago." Her pink tank top didn't meet the waistband of her shorts, leaving an inch of tanned skin exposed. "You have any trouble finding me?"

He smiled at her bare feet and bright red toenails. "No."

"I should've told you I live in a duplex." She gave

his gray slacks a quick frown then took the lead. "What would you like to drink? I have beer, iced tea, orange juice and possibly a couple cans of cola."

John took a look at her tanned legs from the rear and forgot the question. "Uh, what was that?" He followed her through a small room with a floral couch, a black sling-back canvas chair and two tables covered with books. Textbooks. Plants were everywhere, not the decorative artificial variety, but overgrown ferns and glossy-leaved vines that seemed determined to take over the house.

Only a Formica counter crowded with more plants and books separated the room from a tiny galley kitchen. A pair of tall stools sat on the living room side in front of two place mats. A toaster, microwave and blender took up most of the space between the stove and wall on the opposite counter.

Cassie stood at an old white refrigerator that was covered in snapshots and magnets. "What will it be? Oh, I've also got wine. Chardonnay."

"Thanks, but I was hoping to convince you to let me take you out for dinner. You've been working hard lately." He checked out the title of one of the books on the counter. Something about neurology. "And I'm guessing it's not made easier by the fact that you're a student?"

She nodded. "Thanks for the thought, but I invited you to dinner. I didn't think you'd mind staying here. It won't take long to make, and then I've got to hit the books."

"But you don't owe me anything. It was my pleasure

to help out. And it also would be my pleasure to take you to dinner."

"Wow, that's nice, but…"

He glanced again at the textbooks and pads of paper scribbled with notes on the dividing counter. "I suppose me telling you we could go somewhere casual wouldn't convince you?"

"I know it's cluttered and there are lots of plants, but the kitchen's clean." She pushed aside her study material and a potted flowering cactus. "I thought maybe you could quiz me while I cook, but that's okay. Forget it. Dumb idea. In fact, don't feel like you have to stay."

"I didn't mean to imply…"

"I didn't infer anything."

Her arms crossed her chest, and how had this conversation gone so off the rails? He moved around to her side of the counter. "I just wanted you to be waited on for a change," he said. "But I'm happy to help in any way I can. Hell, I'd offer to cook, but that wouldn't be in anyone's best interest."

There was her smile. Wide and bright and making her a whole different kind of pretty. Her hair had something to do with that, and he couldn't deny that outfit of hers was making this nondate thing difficult. He stepped closer to her. Really close, although he didn't touch. "I should lay my cards on the table, though," he said. "Staying here might complicate things."

"How so?" she whispered as her grin disappeared behind a quick swipe of her pink tongue.

Half a step nearer and he watched as her hazel eyes darkened. The temperature of the kitchen had gone up in a flash. "I'm having a lot of difficulty thinking about anything but that kiss of ours."

"That wasn't really about us."

"It may have started out as a game, but it sure didn't end that way. At least for me…" With a gentle nudge of his finger under her chin, he tipped her head back. She stayed perfectly still as he bent to kiss her. As soon as their lips met, her hand came up to rest on his chest.

His body's instant reaction to the kiss shocked him. Last night had obviously been a teaser, because the first taste of her went straight to his cock. Maybe what got to him was the relaxed palm over his heart when she just as easily could have shoved him away. And maybe he'd better back off before things got out of hand.

They broke contact at the same time. He knew why he'd cut the party short, and looked into her face, hoping to learn her reason. He found her staring at her hand, frowning as if it somehow had betrayed her.

"I should start dinner. I've got a test tomorrow, and I'm not ready for it." She met his gaze for a second, then stepped back. "Hope you like pancakes and omelets."

He smiled. He wasn't here for the food. "I think pancakes and omelets sound great."

CASSIE TURNED TO THE FRIDGE. He was damn smooth, and she wasn't used to that. Not when it seemed so earnest. She thought about how he'd offered to leave the bar yesterday, how he'd made sure she came out of the Karma situation on top. It was entirely possible he was for real.

"What did you say you wanted to drink?"

"A beer would be good."

"One beer coming up, Mr.—what is your last name?"

"Devlin."

"Devlin," she repeated softly.

"John Harrington Devlin, to be precise."

After she passed him his drink, she reached up to her high cabinet to fetch the pancake mix. She felt his gaze on her as her tank top rode up, sure he'd seen the tattoo on her hip. She wondered if he would comment on it, but he stayed quiet, leaning against the edge of the counter, just far enough not to get in her way. "John Harrington Devlin," she said, turning to the task at hand. "That sounds—"

"Formal?"

"A bit."

"Imagine if I'd tacked on *the third*."

"Are you?" She'd been hoping to find out a little more about him, and even though she would have to hit the books soon, she wasn't about to let this opportunity pass. "There are two more like you?"

"I'm third in line," he said, then thought a moment. "But we're really different."

"Where are you from?"

"I was born in Maryland, but I lived all over the place. We moved about every two or three years."

"An East Coaster, huh?"

"Not so much. We left Maryland when I was three."

"What about your parents? It counts if they're from the East."

"My mom's from Boston. The colonel—" John twisted the cap off his beer and took a drink. "My father grew up like I did, living on the West Coast, the Midwest, Europe."

"You call him Colonel?"

"Sometimes."

She stayed quiet, rearranging everything to give herself work space. She turned on the electric griddle and put a container of real maple syrup in the microwave. Pancakes were an important food group, and they deserved nothing but the best.

"What about you?" he asked. "Where are you from?"

"Tempe, Arizona, but I grew up like you. We lived everywhere. Not Europe. Just in the States. I've lived here in Vegas the longest. It's been four years."

"Your folks live here, too?"

"Part-time. They're in Oregon right now. But no fair, I wasn't finished with you yet."

"Ask away."

"What about the first John? He would be your grandfather, right?" She measured out the powdered mix, her unsteady hand not exactly precise. "Was he a colonel, too?"

"Uh-huh."

"What branch?"

"Air force." She bent to get the big blue mixing bowl. Her butt bumped his fly.

"Oh." She stiffened. "I didn't know you were there." Her heel came down on his shoe. "Sorry, did I—?"

"No." He put a hand on her bare waist to steady her. Or something. All she felt was the heat of him, his closeness. He was a stealth mover, closing the distance between them without a sound. The contact between them had only lasted a few seconds, and she doubted that the bump behind his fly was anything but a trick of his trousers.

There was one way of finding out. She turned in a

tight circle, his hand staying in contact until it rested on the other side of her waist.

"You know what?" she asked.

He looked hungry, and she didn't think it was for pancakes. "Nope."

Grabbing the front of his shirt, she tugged him down, and he willingly submitted. "You're pretty darn sneaky."

"Yeah, well, you have your moments, too. I imagined this evening going a whole different way."

He was close enough that his warm, slightly beer-tinged breath caressed her lips. "Oh, yeah? And what did you picture happening?"

"A dinner with waiters and candles. Getting to know you. Bringing you back here reasonably close to the agreed-upon time."

"That's it?"

He nodded, and his nose brushed hers.

"That's not so different."

"I never anticipated seeing your tattoo."

"Oh, that one's nothing."

"There are more?" he asked, his mouth curving into a smile.

Returning his grin, she let go of his shirt, cupped the back of his neck and pulled him the rest of the way down. Her breasts pressed to his chest as she leaned into him. He moved his hands to her back, stroking his palms under her top, trailing his fingers along her spine as if he'd be able to find her ink by touch.

She kept the kiss light, pulling back when she still had her wits about her.

He chased after her, but gave it up as his focus

seemed to clear. "Damn. You aren't making this easier, you know."

"What easier?"

His hands slipped out from under her top and he distanced himself from her. "I'm starving. How about those pancakes?"

"Right. Dinner. Have a seat, and I'll make you a couple. How does a cheese omelet sound?"

He made his way to the opposite side of the counter. "Great. Is there anything I can do to help?"

"You can continue telling me about yourself."

"All right, as long as I get to ask you questions, too."

"Absolutely. Now, what about your mom?" Cassie found it a lot easier to pay attention when she concentrated on the cooking. None of it took very long. After being a bartender so long, she was great at multitasking.

When she did take the occasional peeks at John, his gaze was squarely on her. Mostly her face, but sometimes lower. She was used to being looked at, but his attention was different from that of the guys at the bar.

Somehow, she managed not to spill anything or start a fire.

His story was interesting, although she kept waiting for his admission that he was a fighter pilot. What she got instead were the outside pieces of the jigsaw puzzle, which were interesting, but didn't show the full picture.

"You're what, in your early thirties?" she asked.

"Thirty-three."

"How come you're not married? Or maybe you were?"

John shook his head. "Nope. Travel, circumstances.

I'm not against the institution, but it hasn't been in the cards. Not yet, at least. What about you?"

"I'm not married. I haven't even had a serious boyfriend since I was a sophomore undergrad."

"What happened?"

She turned back to the stove to flip his omelet. It would be done in a minute, so she turned on the microwave to heat the syrup. The pancakes were keeping warm in the oven. "We wanted different things," she said.

"Such as?"

"He was a musician. A very good one. Not a superstar soloist or anything, but he was heading for a seat in a major orchestra."

"What does he play?"

"Cello. And guitar, but he was a cellist. Anyway, in his senior year, he joined a band. Playing guitar. And that was the beginning of the end."

"He gave up the orchestra?"

"He did. Which wouldn't have been a huge issue, or at least one we might have worked out, but the band ended up having some success, and they went on tour. He...found a lot to like in that lifestyle."

"Oh."

"Yeah. It wasn't fun." The microwave dinged, she plated the omelet and a few minutes later they were eating. He'd traded in his beer for O.J. and she finally allowed herself to watch him. He ate well. She liked that. Also, he smiled readily, and laughed at her jokes. At his own, too.

Near the end of the meal, his gaze went to her textbook. "So, grad student?"

She nodded. "Psychology at UNLV."

"Know what you're going to do with the degree yet?"

"I want to be a therapist, so I need a master's degree."

"Is that a lifelong dream?"

She had to think about that. "Kind of. I've always been a nurturer. Trying to make things work between people. But I'm not a pushover, either." Except where her brother was concerned, but John didn't need to know that.

They finished off the last of the meal in an easy silence. Altogether, and despite the fact that she'd probably have to kick him out of her house if she wanted to get any studying done, she wouldn't have missed this. Not for anything.

When he got up to collect the plates, they nearly crashed into each other, because she'd gotten up at the same time.

As close as they could be without touching, she looked up into his face. The mood had gone from easy to sizzling in two-point-three seconds.

7

JOHN WANTED HER as badly as he'd wanted a woman in his life. He thought of that fool of a guitar player, then dismissed the idiot when her lips parted.

He wanted to sweep away all the plates on the counter and take her right there. He wanted her sitting at the edge, legs parted, naked from the waist down. He liked the idea of looking up at that pink top of hers, watching her hard nipples rise and fall as he made her insane with his mouth. Damn, he could practically feel her hands in his hair as he brought her to the brink.

His gaze shot to the counter, but his eye caught on her textbook, and he stepped back so quickly he nearly toppled the stool.

"What?"

His hand went to the back of his neck, where he rubbed the tight muscles. "You need to study. Why don't you get your books and I'll take care of the dishes."

Cassie laughed, but it was more surprise than humor. "Wow, you are seriously a man of your word."

"I try to be. Sometimes it's more difficult than others."

"To tell you the truth," she said, her voice gone soft, not quite a whisper, "I wasn't thinking about grades right then."

He adjusted his stance, he hoped not too obviously. "I wasn't, either."

"I'm glad it wasn't only me. But thank you. I appreciate the effort."

"I should get these dishes in the sink."

She looked at her book, then back at him. "Since we're both being very mature about this whole thing, I'm thinking we could handle taking the edge off a little."

"Define *a little*."

"A few kisses?" She moved close enough to slide her palms up his chest. Kissed his chin.

Instead of turning away, filling his hands with plates and forks, he took hold of that slender waist of hers. It took all his willpower to keep on breathing, to not push his hardening erection into her hip, show her what she was doing to him.

"I'm not trying to start anything," she said. "Just a kiss or two to hold me over." Her slow smile brought out interesting colors in her hazel eyes. Her lashes were dark and thick in contrast to the pale skin that almost looked as soft as it felt.

"I won't be responsible for you being unprepared tomorrow." He punctuated the warning with a gentle press of his lips to hers. "That said...we can be sensible...." He came back with purpose, nudging her mouth open, slipping his tongue inside, more deeply than he'd intended.

She swayed backward. The counter helped steady

her, which would have been fine if it weren't for her leaning into his fly, rubbing with just enough friction to push him beyond his limit. He started to move his hips, already feeling the tight coil at the base of his spine that preceded the point of no return.

He froze. His breath came out in ragged puffs against her cheek. "You're making this extremely difficult," he said through gritted teeth. "You want help with the dishes, or do I quiz you?"

"I don't know whether to be impressed by your self-control, or pissed."

"Be both." He turned around. If he could have walked, he'd have gone to hide in the bathroom until the crisis passed. "I sure as hell am."

She didn't make a sound behind him. Which didn't help.

"What's it going to be?" He picked up his orange juice and polished it off in one gulp. He wished it had been something stronger, but scotch didn't exactly go with omelets.

She sighed. "I'll wash," she said, and walked around him to get her book. After a sad shake of her head, she opened the book to the back pages. "Here are a list of questions and answers."

He watched the sink fill with soapy water, ruthlessly shutting down all the reasons he was being an idiot. But he'd been in situations where studying had to take precedence. Even when it was so difficult the only way to settle was to dig his fingers into his thigh muscle until his cock cried uncle. "You know for sure this material will be covered in your exam?"

"Nope, but some of it should." Before she collected

the dishes, she got herself a glass of iced tea and drank that sucker fast.

Evidently, her body temperature had shot up, too. Speaking of which, he'd probably cool off a lot faster if he started reading over the list of questions.

CASSIE FINISHED putting the dishes in the water. She faced forward, although the image of him sitting at her counter, head bent over her book, was so clear in her mind's eye, she wondered how she'd get through the next ten minutes, let alone a few hours.

"Ready?" he asked.

"Shoot."

"These questions all pertain to where emotions originate in the brain. First one—"

God, she was nervous already. "I warned you I don't test well, right?"

"You shouldn't be worried now. This is only prep."

She'd just bet he was one of those guys who never had to study. "Okay, go."

"Resilience."

She knew this one. "Prefrontal cortex."

"Outlook, as in whether you see the glass half-empty or half-full."

"Ventral striatum."

"Two gold stars so far," he said, and she shook her head, annoyed with herself for caring that she got the answers right for him. "Now, let's see…sensitivity to social cues."

She drew a blank.

"Cassie?"

"I'm thinking."

"This refers to facial expressions, tone of voice—"

"I know what social cues are." She hadn't meant to snap. "Fusiform-amygdala."

"Right again." He paused. "Okay to interject my own question?"

Sighing, she turned. "I'm sorry for being grumpy. Please, ask away."

"No apology necessary. I'd be cussing if I had to memorize this stuff. You really need to know this for a psychology degree?" He looked genuinely horrified, and so damn adorable she wanted to hug him. Thank God she was elbow deep in suds.

"No. I was stupid to sign up for the class. It sounded interesting and I couldn't resist, although I should have audited it instead. I don't need the credits, but I can't have a fail on my records."

"Ah, an overachiever."

"Um, no, definitely not, just impulsive. Why are you looking at me like that?" She tried to stare him down but he wouldn't lose the small mystery smile, as if he knew something about her she didn't. It was ridiculous. He was only privy to what she wanted him to know. "Stop it."

"Next question—sensitivity to internal bodily cues."

Oh, perfect…she was experiencing a bunch of those right now. His shoulders were exceptionally broad, and why hadn't she noticed before? She liked watching him tap his finger on the current question while he scanned the bottom of the page. His nails were trimmed and clean and his fingers were exceptionally long without being too slender. Huh.

He glanced up, met her eyes and smiled. "Did you want the example? Or will you bite my head off?"

"I spaced out for a second, but I know this—" She did. She really did. The answer had been on the tip of her tongue before she'd gotten distracted. "Damn it, I had it."

John got up and walked around the counter until he was at her back. "You're too tense," he said, moving his hands to her shoulders. "Try to relax."

"Easy for you to say."

"Right." He used his thumbs at the base of her neck, where she seemed to carry most of the tension. "Drop your chin."

"Ouch."

"You have a knot here."

"I noticed."

He didn't let up. "Breathe slow and deep," he said, his voice a low hypnotic murmur that made her think of other things she liked slow and deep. "You're tensing again."

Ha. No kidding. The thought of him naked in her bed was more than she could hope to handle. She stared down into the sink and focused on the popping bubbles.

"Take longer to breathe out." His deep baritone yanked her back over to the dark side.

She almost told him that trying to relax would work so much better if he stopped speaking. But then she might have to explain how she was letting her libido take over her entire frontal lobe.

"Bet you hold your breath a lot during exams." He moved his hands toward her shoulder blades, sinking his fingers into the muscle and rubbing out the tension.

"Yes, and clench my teeth."

"Like you're doing now?"

"I'm not—" Cassie shuddered and gripped the edge of the counter to keep from pooling into mush on the linoleum floor. This was pretty relaxed for her. He just didn't know it.

"That could be why you test poorly. You let the tension escalate into panic."

"Other way around. I tense and panic because I can't remember the answer." Closing her eyes, she let out a throaty moan and didn't care that it sounded like she'd had an orgasm. "You're good at this."

"Feeling mellower?"

"Oh, yeah."

"The last question…internal bodily cues—where does the sensitivity originate?"

"The visceral organs."

"Bingo."

"Huh. I wasn't even thinking about it."

"I know." His fingers glided up the side of her neck. No, not his fingers, it was his lips and warm breath that whispered against her sensitized skin…his hands continued to knead her shoulders and back.

"You do realize you'll have to come to class with me tomorrow."

He chuckled, the vibration from his mouth making her skin tingle. "Give you a massage while you take your exam?"

"Exactly."

"Talk to your professor and let me know how that works out." He was no longer touching her, she realized with a jolt. His hands and mouth had been on her a second ago.

Cassie spun around so fast she almost lost her balance. "What are you doing?"

"Removing myself from harm's way." He'd already reclaimed his stool and had transferred his attention to the book.

"But—but..."

His eyebrows went up in amusement. "Yes?"

"You have great hands, really, you should do that for a living." She stretched her neck to the side and flexed her shoulders, acutely aware of the ache in her breasts. Damn it, she didn't care about cleaning or studying... she could do those things later. "But if you need more practice, I'm here for you."

John smiled. "That's very kind."

"Yep, that's me. Always willing to take one for the team." She could seduce him. Eventually he'd fold.

"When I was in college I used to choke at key times, myself," he said. "Not consistently, which almost made it worse because I didn't know when I would freeze."

"Here I thought you were one of those people who sailed through school without breaking a sweat."

"I admit, I had it easier than most of my friends. I didn't have to study as much as they did and I tested fine, but I had a couple of problem areas."

"Expectations about your performance?"

He frowned. "What makes you say that?"

"The colonels. Two of them in a row." It was clear she was navigating a minefield. He seemed uneasy, which reinforced the awful thought she'd had earlier. He'd enlisted but hadn't cut it. A failed military career would keep him mum on the subject.

"My family wasn't pushy about me joining the air force. Of course they knew that's what I wanted. If I'd said I planned on being a professional masseur, I imagine they would've had a rather strong opinion."

"A masseur." She grinned, feeling less anxious. He didn't appear to be a man who'd flunked out of the air force after all. "You would've been terrific."

"Guess we'll never know."

She turned back and got washing, finishing the dishes quickly, and moving on to the bowl and measuring cup. "So, are you still in the service?"

"Yep, stationed right here at Nellis."

"Are you a colonel?"

He laughed. "A captain. I'm only thirty-three."

"What's next?"

"I'm up for major."

"Then colonel?"

He hesitated, and curious, she turned to look at him, but he wasn't at the counter. Instead, he'd gone to the fridge and pulled out a beer. He glanced at her, but didn't say anything until he'd gotten back on the stool and was able to take a swig off the bottle. Finally, he shrugged. "If I stay in long enough,"

"That was a joke, right?" She kept swirling the sponge in the batter bowl, but couldn't stop looking at him. "I mean, you must be halfway to retirement by now, unless my math is wrong."

"You're right on both counts."

She didn't believe him. At least not about the joking part. Why make light of something like that? His family would, as he'd put it, have a strong opinion. "You must be on leave."

"For another week."

"And you stayed here? It's broiling. Are you crazy?"

He leaned back, confidence oozing from his smile, his shoulders taking up so much room he looked as if he owned the place. "And aren't you glad I did?"

Cassie gave him a long look. "The cockiness finally surfaces."

"I meant that I'm here to help you study." He was clearly annoyed with her comment. "Finally surfaces? What does that mean?"

"You pilots are a different breed."

"I didn't say I was a pilot."

"But you are…" She grinned with her own brand of smug. "Aren't you?"

John kept staring at her but he didn't respond. Was he still pissed about her remark? That didn't seem like him. He had a sense of humor and was a good sport. The kiss at the bar proved that.

"I should've taken Lisa's bet." Cassie stopped and thought a moment. "No, she wanted to bet on whether you'd leave after your first sip of scotch. She wouldn't have put money on whether you were air force or a pilot. We both knew you were a flyboy the moment you walked in."

"Is it the haircut?" His flat tone felt off.

"That might've had something to do with it, though your hair's a bit longer than most airmen. I think mainly it's the swagger." She saw straight off that she'd used the wrong word. Or maybe he'd interpreted it as something negative, because the firm set of his mouth said he wasn't pleased. "But not in a bad way. I'm not in any way dissing you. So you're a pilot…I think that's fine."

He let out a short surprised laugh. "Huh," he said. "I appreciate it." He shook his head, his amused expression a relief. "Those men who sit in the corner with your pal Gordon. They say anything?"

"Not to me. Why?"

"I noticed a couple of retired lifers in the group. Those guys aren't always happy to share their space with officers."

"The retirees aren't the problem," she said. "It's the others who came back wounded. Not all of them, just the guys looking for someone to blame. I can't pretend I understand what they went through, but I get that it's easier to be angry than frightened."

"Including your brother?"

"He was wounded in Iraq," she said quietly, and rinsed the last of the utensils.

"Sorry, I shouldn't have asked."

"No, it's fine." She unplugged the sink and turned around to wipe her hands. "You've probably heard Tommy's story a hundred times. An IED took out half his unit and part of his leg. But he's lucky. He has Lisa, who loves him even though he can be a complete ass, and he has the bar. It's not exactly a gold mine, despite the name, but it generates a few bucks and allows him to be his own boss. Which, if you knew my brother, is a major advantage because his attitude sucks and he never shows up when he's supposed to. He was fitted with a new prosthetic a few weeks ago—did I already tell you?"

She frowned, trying to remember. "No, when could

I have done that...? Anyway, the first one had been a bear for him, he won't even give this one a fair chance. He could have a pretty normal life. But nooo...he'd rather bitch and moan about how it doesn't feel right. Now, when I see him coming through the door in his old wheelchair, I could just throw—"

She drew in a quick breath, startled at how she'd gone off, ranting like a lunatic. It unsettled her that she'd been staring at John but not really seeing him. She did now, and she felt foolish. Maybe she should've found comfort in his sympathetic brown eyes, but she had no business talking about Tommy. God, she didn't really know John. This wasn't like her.

"Aren't you glad you asked?" she muttered, pushing her hands through her hair and fixing her gaze on the countertop.

"Yeah, I am." His voice seemed closer, and she dared to slide him a look. He'd left the stool and was coming toward her. "You forgot something."

"What?"

"Tommy has you."

"Does that go in the plus or minus column?"

John put his arms around her. "I assume that's rhetorical."

"Not really. I should be helping him to live an independent life instead of enabling him." She closed her eyes, enjoying the feel of his chest under her palms, his arms around her back. "Technically I'm the one who'll be leaving, but he has to be able to stand on his own."

"Do you think he can?"

"I know he can, but he doesn't believe it. I think he's in denial about me leaving after school."

"Good thing he has Lisa." John tucked her head under his chin and stroked her back.

"If he doesn't blow it. She loves him, but she has her limits." Cassie didn't know John well enough to feel this safe and content with her cheek pressed to his heart. If anything she should feel guilty for not shutting up. But she hadn't realized how much she'd bottled up and it felt good to unload. There was only so much she could say to Lisa. For as long as she'd known Gordon and Spider and some of the others, Cassie would never have this conversation with one of them.

Sadly, she couldn't even discuss Tommy with her parents. They cared, of course, but in an odd, detached way. She'd never really understood them. Other than the fact that they put each other first, and she and Tommy came second. It wasn't a guess. When Cassie was ten, her mother had come out and said as much.

"When the time comes, will you be ready to cut the strings?" John asked, his breath stirring her hair.

"Absolutely." She looked up at him. "I hope."

"Luckily, today you don't have to think about that. But you do have to study."

"Here I was thinking we could've spent all this time kissing." Her stomach did a flip-flop at his strained smile. Had she ruined everything by complaining about Tommy?

John left her at the counter. While she finished straightening the rest of the kitchen, he quizzed her. He kept their focus narrow, and kissed her only once more. On the cheek, on his way out the door.

8

"Wow, YOU MUST NOT have done laundry in a while."
Beth reached across the bar and grabbed one of the
bowls of pretzels Cassie was filling. "You look nice. I
don't think I've ever seen you in anything but a T-shirt."

"Yep, gotta get to the Laundromat," Cassie muttered.
Not true, but this was the fourth time she'd been accused
of not washing her clothes, or something to that effect.

It had started off with Lisa, and since Cassie was ir-
ritable from too little sleep, insufficient studying and
the certainty she'd totally messed up her exam, she'd
decided not to tell Lisa about having John over last
night. Of course it was childish. Keeping Lisa in the
dark hardly served as a punishment, since Lisa didn't
know she was missing out on anything. Somehow it
made Cassie feel better anyway.

Besides, if she did talk to Lisa, then she'd have to
admit she had no idea where things stood between her
and John. Even worse, not knowing bothered her far
too much. Especially because it was 10:00 p.m. and he
hadn't shown up.

He never had asked for her phone number, or volunteered his. While he knew where she lived and worked, she only knew he was a captain stationed at Nellis and that was it. He obviously wanted the information flowing one way, and she was annoyed at herself for bothering to iron her yellow cotton sleeveless blouse just in case he'd show up for a beer.

Damn it, she should've dragged him to bed last night while she'd had the chance. She might as well have, considering he was the reason she'd probably get a C.

The beginning of the test had gone off without a hitch. Then panic had crept in, which she'd actually managed by focusing on her breathing and trying to relax. But that had reminded her of John's lips and hands on her body and, poof, she'd been toast.

God, she wanted him to come by if only to tell him thanks for nothing. Sighing, she brought out a shot glass and grabbed the bottle of tequila. This was every bit her fault. She'd broken her own rule and it was costing her. Big-time. Even if she had made plans with John, it wouldn't have meant anything. Not in the long run. He was on leave. That explained so much.

Which was fine. Because as soon as school was over, she was out of here. Maybe they would've only had a week, but man, what a week it could have been.

Lisa plopped down her tray. "I hate it when we're this slow. Feels like I've been here for three days instead of four hours. Where the hell is everybody, anyway?"

"Barbecues and softball games. The hospital gang has some sort of tournament going on."

"I don't understand doing things outside when it's three thousand degrees."

"You and me both, sister."

"Oh, honey, you know as well as I do June is nothing compared to July and August." Lisa's gaze flicked over Cassie's button-down blouse. "That looks cute on you. Bet you have a good tip night." She grinned, then looked over at the empty stool where John normally sat. "Where's flyboy?"

"How should I know?" Heat flooded Cassie's cheeks, and she ducked to get the cut-up limes out of the mini-fridge. Lisa stared curiously at her for a few seconds, then got distracted by the shot of booze sitting in front of Cassie. Lisa's gaze darted to her order pad. "Did I forget to deliver a drink?"

"Nope, this is for me."

"Seriously?" Lisa blinked extravagantly as she watched Cassie prepare her salt and lime. "Your exams must be finished."

"I have one more, and then I'm done until September." She decided to skip the lime and salt and downed the tequila, cringing when she shuddered like an amateur.

"You never drink while you're working."

"I do occasionally...when it's slow."

Lisa eyed her suspiciously. For good reason—because it was true. Cassie hardly ever drank at the bar. It seemed she was always anxious to get home, always studying, always stressed.

"You should be able to leave early if you want," Lisa said, giving the room a quick look-see, but no one was signaling for service. "It was like this last night. Of course your brother bitched because, well, he's Tommy, but we had no trouble keeping up. Lots of beer drinkers, so that helped."

"Yeah, I'll probably shove off in the next hour." The words were barely out of her mouth when the door opened. With a weird certainty that it was John, she turned a casual glance that way. It wasn't him. Two guys who were kind of familiar walked up to the bar.

She and Lisa greeted the men with smiles, but Cassie was too disappointed to fake it well. Behind her the phone rang. Another waste of money. Hardly anyone called the landline anymore, but Tommy insisted on being listed in the Yellow Pages.

Lisa started to come around the bar to answer the phone, but Cassie motioned for her to take the customers' order. She'd get a better tip out of the men. Cassie was just too damn grumpy to go that extra mile.

"Gold Strike," she said, her greeting close to a bark.

"Cassie?"

She recognized John's voice, and immediately turned to face the wall for a teeny bit of privacy. "Hey."

"Are you busy?"

"No, slow tonight."

"Yeah, even the parking lot is half-empty."

Abruptly she looked at the door. "Where are you?"

"Just outside, sitting in my car."

"Oh." She glanced down at her top, grateful beyond words she'd done a quick fix with club soda on a spot of tomato juice that had splashed her earlier. "Why?"

"Any chance you'll get off early?"

"Yes, and again, why?" She'd tried to sound casual, as if his call was no big deal, but it wasn't working. Her pulse had started racing at the sound of him, which was not a good sign. A smart woman would make an excuse and hang up, not keep ignoring all the signs that she was already in over her head. Instead, she said, "You owe me two answers."

John's deep laugh made everything worse because she could picture the smile that went with it. "You up for a party?"

She watched Lisa fill a mug with beer and chat with the men. "*Party* being a euphemism for…?"

"Uh…" He trailed off to a brief silence. "No hats, no balloons, but it really is a party."

"Where?"

"A friend's house, about twenty minutes from here. By the way, I want to know how your exam went, but I figured we'd talk on the drive. If you want to join me."

For all her internal lecturing, Cassie wanted to see him. She wouldn't pretend otherwise, but hanging out at a party with his friends wasn't what she had in mind.

"I promised I'd show up," he said, as if sensing her hesitation. "We don't have to stay long."

"I'm thinking."

"Should I come in? I thought you wouldn't want me asking in front of customers."

"You're right." She glanced down at herself. The top would do, but the old jeans were horrible. "Maybe you should go ahead on your own. I'd have to go home and change and—"

"Nah, it's not like that. They barbecued earlier, and now it's drinks and snacks around the pool. You're dressed fine."

"You don't know what I'm wearing."

"But I know you look good," he said, his voice low and smoky.

Smiling, she realized she was twisting her hair

around her finger like a smitten thirteen-year-old and snapped out of it. Damn. Lisa was watching her. "Give me ten minutes."

He might've said something about waiting on the street instead of the parking lot, but she'd pretty much hung up on him.

Avoiding Lisa's gaze, Cassie muttered, "I'll be right back," then grabbed her purse and hurried to the ladies' room for some damage control. Nothing to do about her clothes, but her hair and makeup probably needed touching up.

If she made it out the door without having to field a dozen questions from Lisa and Tommy, it would be a miracle. And then all she had to do was survive the night with John. No problem. Though another shot of tequila might be just the ticket.

"Cassie, this is Shane and Nancy, our hosts." John kissed the woman's cheek, while Cassie smiled and shook hands with her husband.

She should've known better. The rule was a basic one, for God's sake. Never trust a man when it came to his opinion on clothes. Even if he swore you looked like a million bucks. Of course John hadn't used those words, but he'd assured her she looked perfect. Wrong. Wrong. Wrong.

"Glad you guys could make it." Shane glanced at the label on the wine John had given him, his brows arching in approval. "Too bad you missed dinner. We should have some leftover steak and chicken. Honey, how about bringing out the—"

"No, not for us...." John pressed a hand to Cassie's

lower back. "I'm sorry, I shouldn't speak for you, Cass." He looked into her eyes, his dazzling smile for her alone. "Hungry?"

His touch startled her as much as the nickname. He stood close, the pressure of his palm steady, and anyone watching would think they'd known each other for a whole lot longer than four days.

Okay, she could forgive him for not warning her that she'd look like a toad next to all these gorgeous women. There was an assortment of blondes, brunettes and even two redheads lounging around the pool, or talking and laughing under the small palm trees strung with hundreds of white glittering lights. The landscaping was primo, with lots of trees and flowering shrubs, and a ton more lighting.

"Cassie?" John rubbed his thumb near her spine.

"Oh, sorry. Yes." She looked blankly at him, then to Nancy and Shane. "I mean, no. Not hungry. But thanks."

"Let me know if you change your mind. It's really no trouble." Nancy was a blonde, and damn, a natural one it seemed. Very nice. Very tall. Stunning, actually, dressed in white capris and a white strappy top. "Excuse me, I have to check on the ice."

"You know where the bar is," Shane told John. "Help yourself," he said, with a smile for Cassie before he followed Nancy toward the covered patio.

Cassie stared after him. He had dark hair like John, same height, gorgeous blue eyes, but John was still much better-looking. "They seem nice."

"You sound surprised."

"Do I?" She turned to see him smiling at her. But her move forced him to break contact, and she was sorry about that. "I don't know why. I can't imagine you hanging out with jerks."

His grin broadened. "How about a drink? This time I'm pouring."

"Yes, you are." She hesitated when he gestured for her to go first. "Which way's the bar?"

"The patio, left of the sliding doors."

She'd been kind of hoping he'd take her hand, but that was expecting too much. At least they didn't have to circle the pool. Most of the guests mingled over on the other side, but that hadn't stopped the curious looks aimed at her and John. He nodded to a woman sitting at the edge of a lounge chair, then slowed to tell a couple of guys—had to be pilots—he'd catch up with them in a minute.

"Do you know everyone here?" Cassie leaned on the high bamboo bar, watching him make her a tequila sunrise. He'd set out the right ingredients, plus lime juice for some reason.

He glanced out at the pool and the couples sitting at the umbrella tables. "About half. I work with most of the guys. I think the two couples talking by the diving board are neighbors."

"Are the women wives, or what?" She was careful not to stare because some of the women were looking back, and in fact had been watching her and John since they arrived. Hard to tell if they were curious about her or bummed that John hadn't come solo. Probably both.

"A few wives," he said, returning his attention to her drink. "I think the rest are Nancy's friends."

"Jeez, they all look like models."

"They could be." He was so careful to measure everything precisely it made her smile.

"Notice something else?"

His head came up again, his gaze going from her to the pool, back to her. "What?"

"None of them are wearing jeans."

"The guys are. Including me."

"That's different."

"How?" After taking in her face and hair, he looked directly into her eyes, his lips lifting in the faintest of smiles as if they shared a secret.

A shiver of pure pleasure danced up her spine. Bless him for making her feel as if she were the only woman at this shindig. "You know what—forget it."

He handed her the tequila sunrise. "Tell me if I made this right. You're the expert."

"An expert at what?" The man's voice behind her was close enough to make her jump.

She stepped aside so she could turn to look without bumping into him. He brushed her arm, making her tense until he lifted his hands in apology.

"Sorry, didn't mean to startle you." He held an empty glass that should stay that way, judging by his flushed face and bloodshot blue eyes.

"Rocky." John gave him a polite nod but she got a negative vibe. "I didn't know you were here."

"John meant that he didn't know I was invited," he said, winking at Cassie, his attention focused on her. "Introduce me to your girl, Devil."

"I haven't been a girl in a decade." She decided she didn't want to shake his hand but she wouldn't be rude. "I'm Cassie," she said, then glanced at John. "Devil?"

"Call sign." His grim expression made it clear he didn't want to explain further. Not now anyway. "His name is Kevin."

Kevin set his glass on the bar, then somehow stumbled over his own foot, nearly knocking the glass over. He just laughed and said, "Scotch-rocks for me, bartender."

John cleared his throat. He didn't seem upset, just trying to keep a straight face. "You driving?"

"I'm not drunk, so don't worry about it."

"There you are." Nancy came from behind Kevin and slipped her arm through his. "I haven't talked to you all night."

"Nancy." Kevin gave her a sloppy grin. "My favorite hostess. Where's that son-of-a-bitch husband of yours? I hope far away."

"I'm a bit warm. Mind if we sit inside?" She smoothly steered him toward the glass doors and mouthed a thank-you to John and Cassie.

John waited until they were in the house to turn and catch Cassie's arm. His kiss surprised her. It was brief, but no less shocking. Someone had to have seen them. Speechless, she gazed at him, and he looked as if he might've surprised himself. "You really do look beautiful." Lowering his head to peer at her through his lashes, he said, "Believe me?"

"Hmm, not really. You may have to repeat it." Her bluff would've been more effective without the nervous laugh.

Amusement gleamed in his eyes. "Now or later?"

Neither of them had checked to see if anyone was watching.

She elbowed him, then sipped her drink. "This is good, by the way." She glanced at the sliding doors, hoping Nancy's evening hadn't been ruined. "Does Kevin work with you?"

"Indirectly." His expression tightened. "He doesn't fly anymore. In a few months he'll have put in his twenty and he's out."

"I thought he looked older than the rest of you." She glanced across the pool. Funny how the guys all seemed to share a certain image—physically fit, yes, but also the way they carried themselves. Nobody would mistake them for ordinary airmen. Kevin was different. He looked...soft. "Would you say most people retire after they reach the magic number?"

"Not necessarily. Depends what their military job is and whether they have something else lined up in advance." He sipped his beer, and she followed his gaze toward the backyard.

A willowy blonde wearing tight leggings under a filmy tunic waved to him. She'd been one of the women who'd sporadically kept an eye on John.

Like the men, the women shared a particular image. And like Kevin, Cassie was odd person out. She wondered if John was thinking the same thing.

"I know it's early but do you have plans for a second career?"

"I don't want to talk shop, you mind?"

"No, of course not. I shouldn't have asked." She knew better. Talk about ignoring social cues. His body language had shifted and tension had transformed his expression. Though that might still be a reaction to Kevin.

"Hey, you can ask me anything." He shrugged. "I

may not have an answer, but I'll tell you what I can. Come on, we should go mingle."

She was not looking forward to rubbing elbows with the beautiful people. No offense to them. Maybe if she weren't wearing jeans... No, that had nothing to do with it. But these were his friends and his party, and she'd signed up for date duty the minute she agreed to come. With a smile, she said, "Lead on."

"Thanks," he whispered.

Cassie had no idea what the gratitude was for, and she didn't care. Especially not when his big warm hand closed around hers.

9

JOHN DISCREETLY CHECKED his watch. How could they only have been here an hour? It didn't seem possible. But then he was impatient to be alone with Cassie, so yeah, time was dragging.

Since she seemed to be enjoying herself, he hadn't suggested they leave yet.

As they mingled, sipping drinks, stopping for introductions and hellos, he couldn't help notice the reactions being sent his way when Cassie wasn't looking. Frankly, he was getting annoyed with the inquisitive eyebrow lifts from his fellow pilots and their plus-ones.

They paused near the deep end of the pool and Cassie got roped into a conversation about the correct way to make mojitos. As he took his next sip, listening to Cassie's conversation with the female half of Shane's neighbors, his eye caught on Nancy huddled with her friend Carolyn. He'd always liked Shane's wife, but he was tired of her trying to fix him up. The beautiful and polished Carolyn, case in point. Then there was Rick's date. She'd brought her sister—another attempt at matchmaking. So naturally Rick gave him the stink eye before pointedly frowning at Cassie.

John didn't give a damn. His night wasn't going according to plan, either. A few hours ago, he'd decided to skip the party altogether. The chance to see Cassie outside the bar changed his mind.

Next to him, she laughed and the warmth he felt for her, aside from the want that had been on simmer since that first day at the bar, made him glad that he'd brought her.

In the company of his friends, he felt adrift. In Cassie, a lifeline.

What the hell was going on with him?

Last night, after the frustration of being thoroughly decent for Cassie's sake, he'd found himself caught up in memories of another decent man. His friend Danny. He and Sam and Danny had been a team since college. John's thoughts had kept him up late—dark, circular and confusing thoughts. The tragedy of Danny's death was something John fought to understand. It had been so senseless. Danny hadn't made any mistakes. The fault had been in the jet. Something had gone wrong with two things that weren't even parts of the same system. Completely unrelated. Neither of which should have happened at all, let alone at the same time.

And like that, Danny was gone, leaving his wife, his friends, his future.

As if obsessing over Danny hadn't been hellish enough, John's brain had insisted on replaying Sam's phone call when he'd confessed that he'd been grounded. After surgery to correct his vision had somehow gone wrong, his eyesight had slipped just enough to ruin his career. By the time John had spoken to him, Sam had gotten his act together and tried to sound upbeat about his new plan. But underneath the forced calm, John had heard the devastation in his friend's voice, had felt Sam's bone-deep pain as clearly as if it had been his own. *Never allowed in the cockpit again.* The idea was unthinkable.

The morbid train of thought made its own kind of sense, he supposed. Helping Cassie study brought up memories of him and his friends. The three of them had been decidedly different yet they'd bonded over their passion for flying. They'd crammed for exams together, pushed each other to be better, stronger, smarter, even when the course load got so tough it would've been easy to switch dreams.

Damn it, John had no right to be judging the people at this party, no right to question his own amazing good fortune. Danny had given his life. Sam had soldiered on, willing to become an instructor instead of a pilot, when being a pilot was all he'd lived for.

It was easy to look down his nose at officers like Kevin who drank too much and screwed other officers' wives. But John was guilty as well of too little gratitude for too much privilege.

Cassie's tug on his shirt alerted him that he was about to guide them right into the pool. He hadn't even realized they'd been walking, or where to.

She didn't seem to mind. She smiled at him the same way she had in the Gold Strike and in her tiny overgrown kitchen. It was the first time in years that he hadn't specifically sold himself as an air force pilot. That had always been his calling card, and it worked an amazing amount of the time. But Cassie didn't care. When she looked at him she didn't see the flight suit, just the man. She'd even promised she wouldn't hold it against him.

"You've been awfully quiet," she said.

"I apologize. I'm being a terrible date. I should be showing you off—"

"I'd rather talk with you."

Before he could muster a response to that, a call came from near the house.

"John? Over here."

He recognized Moony's wife's high-pitched voice before he spotted her waving him and Cassie over. But her name escaped him. He motioned that they'd join them, then he squeezed Cassie's hand. Her lips tilted up at the corners and her eyes sparkled. No drink demands or an open textbook to distract her. She looked happy and relaxed, and he felt better than he had all day.

He wanted to kiss her. Sweep her away to somewhere private. But that would have to wait for a bit. "You're about to meet two couples. Mike, known as Moony, and Scott, whose call sign is the uninventive Scotty, are in my squadron. Scotty's wife is Ashley but I can't remember Mike's wife's name so work with me."

"Got it."

Inevitably they were stopped twice on their way to the group by the house. The few who hadn't already gaped at John's companion made no effort to hide their stares. True, he rarely brought a woman to a party, but these idiots should know better than to be obvious. Cassie had to be aware of what was going on, but she was the picture of grace. She smil<u>ed</u> a lot and sipped her tequila sunrise.

"I wondered why you asked me to come," she whispered once they had a clear shot to Mike and company. "Now I know."

"How's that?"

"To save you from all these women."

"Half of them are married."

"Trust me," she said, with a soft laugh. "You have enough to worry about with the other half."

"Wrong, Freud, there are lots of single guys here." He grinned at her warning squint, then leaned in until his lips brushed her earlobe. "I brought you because you're hot."

"Stop it." She shook her head, color blossoming in her cheeks. "I'll give you ten minutes, and that's it, you have to stop or face the consequences."

Chuckling, he let go of her hand and slid his arm around her shoulders. She didn't seem to mind, if her snuggle was anything to go by. His own reaction could turn into a problem if he wasn't careful. He'd give the party a half hour, and that was it. "Let's not stay long, huh?"

"That's fine," she said. "I can think of a few things we could do instead."

A few steps from the foursome, he looked down into her oh-so-innocent gaze. "You telling me you don't have one more test to study for?"

"That's what I meant. Studying."

"Like hell."

"Fine, so I might have been referring to something a little more...naked," she said under her breath, then turned a bright smile to the others as she approached with an extended hand. "Hi, I'm Cassie."

It was that easy. Everyone introduced themselves, and John remembered Gwen's name the second he heard it. He also remembered that he didn't care for her. In fact, he'd been shocked when Mike married her last year after they'd met in a casino bar five months earlier. She was pretty, but an obvious social climber, and everything from her bottle-blond hair to her red nails was fake. So were her breasts. She wore blouses cut low enough for anyone to notice. That would have been fine, if she hadn't made it perfectly clear that she'd married Mike only because he was a pilot.

"Is everything all right with Kevin?" Gwen asked, and Jesus, even her concern was fake.

"Yes, I think so." Cassie smiled and sipped.

Gwen eyed her with a glint of suspicion. "I saw Nancy walking him into the house."

Cassie refused to take the bait. Clearly she knew the woman was looking for dirt, and Cassie didn't want to play in her sandbox. Good for her.

"So what are you doing with your time off?" Mike asked him. "Golfing?"

"Not a golfer. I used to play tennis once a week, but I haven't for a while."

"I knew it," Cassie said, and everyone looked at her. She gave a sheepish shrug. "Your forearms," she muttered, and gestured vaguely. "They're muscular. Like a tennis player's."

Mike laughed and leaned forward to make a comment, but his voice died as his wife reached over and rubbed a hand up and down John's right arm. "Oooh, you're right. Very nice. Keep that up."

The sudden silence that fell seemed louder than a sonic boom. Mike frowned at Gwen, then at John. He'd already stepped back, but the moment was no less awkward.

"I know you guys are stationed at Nellis," Cassie said, moving closer to John, her expression neutral, her voice pleasant and even. She smoothed over the gaffe like a pro. "But where are you all from?"

"Scott and I grew up outside of Dallas," Ashley said. "We went to the same high school, but we didn't actually meet until after college."

"Totally by accident," Scott added, smiling at his wife. "I was home on leave and went to a buddy's wedding."

"I was one of the bridesmaids." Ashley leaned into him. "We didn't even know we'd gone to the same school until we talked that evening."

"More like the whole night." Scott slipped an arm around her waist. "Two years later everyone came to *our* wedding."

Cassie sighed. "That is so sweet."

John hadn't heard the story before, but he knew Scott was crazy about his wife. He talked to her twice a day even when they'd been in the thick of things in Kabul. Watching them look at each other he felt that weird pull in his chest again.

"I'm from Vegas," Gwen said, her high-pitched voice even more annoying now. "Born and raised. Everyone is always surprised. For some reason they think the Strip is all there is, that real people don't actually live here." She fanned her face and cleavage. "God, it's hot. Cassie, what do you do?"

"I'm a bartender."

Gwen's eyebrows shot up. "Really?"

"Really."

"Where? On the Strip?"

"No, a small dive bar my brother owns."

"So you must be from here," Gwen said, taking in Cassie's jeans and black flip-flops.

"Nope. But I've lived here longer than anyplace else, so it kind of feels like home." Cassie stirred what remained of her drink.

John thought about offering to get her another, but he preferred they leave. Figuring it was a safe bet she'd agree, he waited for his chance at a graceful exit. He didn't need Mike to think they were running off because John felt guilty about what had happened. That was on Gwen, and it was between her and Mike.

"Are you a military brat?" Gwen asked. "Is that why you moved around?"

"No, my parents were...well, they still are...bikers."

"Did you say *bikers?*" Gwen's gaze narrowed with curiosity first at Cassie, and then at John. "As in Hell's Angels?"

John tried not to show his hand but he was surprised. He wasn't sure why.... What her parents did had nothing to do with Cassie, except, what a life for a child.

Cassie smiled. "No. We rode with different groups over the years, but mostly for social and safety reasons."

"So you traveled with them even as a kid?"

"Yep. Me and my brother each had our own sidecar."

Gwen had moved closer, her pitch climbing higher and drawing attention. "What about school? You poor thing...did you even get an education?"

John saw Mike tense at the condescension in his wife's voice.

Cassie didn't appear bothered, but then she had a good poker face. "My mom homeschooled us. She was a teacher before she met my father and took up the lifestyle, and she was strict about study time. So we had a better education than most public school kids."

"But how do you know—?"

"Honey, mind getting me another drink?" Mike put his empty glass in Gwen's hand. With a pointed look, he sent her a message to back off, which she ignored.

"Were you able to make friends?" Gwen asked, sidling up to Cassie and touching her arm as if she were her new best friend.

"Too many, I'm afraid. In forty-two states. I'm terrible at answering emails." Cassie smiled. "I'll go with you to get drinks. Any takers? I'm a damn good bartender."

Scott accepted the offer, but only for a beer. John declined, and so did Ashley, who seemed torn between volunteering to go and staying put, out of Gwen's reach. The woman had managed to make everyone uncomfortable. Though not Cassie. Not that she was about to put Gwen on speed dial, but Cassie had taken control, diffused the awkward situation without anyone the wiser. Except for him, but he was starting to understand her. And she was really something.

"They don't need another pair of hands," he said

quietly to Ashley, who looked as if she might cave in to guilt.

She winced. "You sure?"

Staring after Cassie, he smiled. "I'm sure."

"HONEY, I'M SO GLAD you came tonight." Gwen tilted her head toward Cassie and lowered her voice as they passed a foursome sitting at a table. "You're going to need my help. Look, I get where you're coming from, I do." Letting out a weary sigh, Gwen's gaze swept the front of Cassie's jeans and blouse. "Believe it or not, I used to dress like you. But, honey, you aren't going to bag a fighter pilot, let alone a man like John Devlin—" she gestured with her hand, glossy red nails slicing through the air "—looking like this."

Cassie almost missed her cue. She glanced down at her disreputable jeans and inexpensive blouse, then looked up into her self-appointed fairy godmother's face. "Could you define *bag?*"

"What?"

"You said, 'bag a fighter pilot.' What does that mean?"

Impatience flashed in Gwen's eyes. "You know. Get him to marry you."

"That's sweet," Cassie said. "You're sweet, really. But I don't want to marry John. I just want him for sex."

She grabbed a beer for Scott, then walked straight toward John, so tall and lean and looking ridiculously handsome in his jeans and blue polo shirt. He was by far the hottest guy at the party...not that she was biased. What she'd liked best was that he hadn't batted an eye over her parents being bikers or that she herself had lived on the road, even though it was clear she'd sur-

prised him. And when she'd told his friends she was a
bartender, he hadn't tried to mitigate it by adding she
was a grad student.

"I decided not to have another drink," she said after
giving Scott his beer. She latched on to John's arm and
leaned close so the others couldn't hear. Cassie stood
on her toes, and whispered, "I hope you don't mind. I
told Gwen I just wanted you for sex."

John laughed and coughed at the same time.

The other three turned to see what was going on,
and Cassie just smiled.

"I'm not gonna ask how that came up."

"That's smart." She shifted her weight so that the
side of her breast pressed against his arm. "So…when
were you thinking of leaving?"

He studied her face for a long, heated moment. "Your
place okay?"

She nodded, tried to look blasé, then saw the wild
pulse in his neck. Despite the warm flush surging to
her cheeks she shivered.

"Hey, we're going to be moving on. I'll see you guys
later," John said, putting his arm around her and turning her back toward the house.

"You leaving?" Mike asked, and Scott grinned.
"Something we said?"

"I think it was something I said." Smiling, Cassie
wiggled her fingers. "Nice meeting you."

HANDS STUFFED in his pockets so he wouldn't do something foolish like maul her in front of her neighbors,
John waited while Cassie fumbled with her keys. He
would've been more impatient if not for the distraction

of the overhead porch light shimmering off the golden highlights in her hair. No ponytail tonight, just long loose shiny curls that fell past her shoulders.

She had great skin. Soft, smooth, some freckles that seemed to blend with her light tan. He'd find them, though, each and every one, once they got inside the duplex. And her tattoos. It was crazy, but he looked forward to discovering where they were hidden...if she ever got the door unlocked.

"Need help?"

"I almost have it." She shoved with her free hand. "Here we go." She flipped on a light switch as she stepped inside.

"Does the door always stick?"

"Mostly in the summer."

"Remind me to have a look at it."

She turned to face him, a slow smile lifting the corners of her mouth. "You surprise me. Not many people do."

"I didn't say I could fix it." He closed the door behind him. "I just said I'd look at it."

Cassie threw her purse and keys at a chair. The purse landed safely, the keys thudded on the floor. "Ha. You're a riot. You want something to drink?"

"I'm good."

"I'll be the judge of that." Grinning, she pulled the hem of his shirt from his jeans and tugged him toward her.

"So you just want me for sex, huh?"

"I'm sorry." She laughed. "I am. But Gwen, she's just—well, she's kinda nuts. Have she and Mike been married long?"

"No." He kissed her bare shoulder and slid a finger down her chest to the first of far too many little white buttons.

"Right." She briefly closed her eyes and slid her palms up his chest. "We won't talk about them."

"Good."

"Come." She took his hand and led him to the hall opposite the side of the kitchen.

They passed a small bedroom on the left, a bathroom on the right. Her bedroom was at the end, the walls painted a light blue, the queen-size bed neatly made and covered by a puffy white comforter. The room wasn't crowded like the rest of the house. A small dresser stood beside an old-fashioned sliding-door closet. No clothes were strewn around. Some were folded inside a plastic laundry basket sitting in the corner on the floor.

On her dresser were two small green plants. In front of them a pair of goldfish swam in a bowl. It made John smile.

She followed his gaze. "Oh, that's Heart and Soul." She kicked off her flip-flops, then moved one of the plants in front of the bowl. "Don't worry, I won't let the kids watch."

Shaking his head, he toed of his deck shoes. He was willing to wager she surprised him a whole lot more than he surprised her.

Her lips parted as she watched him pull off his shirt then toss it aside.

John caught her upper arms and held her still while he kissed the side of her neck. He skimmed his lips against her silken skin and said, "Now, you just stand there and look gorgeous while I do all the work."

10

CASSIE TOUCHED HIS CHEST with the reverence it deserved. So much warm flesh, hard muscle; the man took care of himself. She drew her hand down to his belly, flat and firm with just enough muscle to keep it that way. "Do you have to work out for your job?"

"Cassie?"

It wasn't easy…she had so much to look at…but she lifted her gaze. His eyes were dark and full of purpose. "What?"

He raised his hands. "I can't unbutton you while you're doing that."

"Give me a minute."

"It's just a chest," he said. "Every guy has one."

She laughed, which didn't help either her exploration of his chest or the unbuttoning of her blouse.

John looked down at her with one raised brow.

"After you have more blood going north, you'll understand," she said. Then she took over button duty, enjoying the view as John undid his belt.

"Done." She let her blouse fall to the floor and smiled in victory. The raw hunger in his eyes made her swallow, though, and flex her hands as she fought the urge to cover herself. Although why she'd want to do that when he approved so demonstrably, she'd never understand.

His gaze skimmed her bare breasts, swept up to her face and surprisingly stayed there. He touched her cheek before lifting a lock of her hair. Smiling, he watched the strands sift through his fingers. His focus returned to her breasts. As he rubbed his thumb over her hard nipple she could see the struggle for control in the flex of his jaw and his flaring nostrils.

"I knew they'd be perfect," he murmured, and kissed her shoulder as his hands moved down to her jeans.

Arousal flushed her entire body. The feel of his warm lips brushing soft kisses up the side of her neck made her dizzy. When he retraced the path and headed for her right breast, she clung to his waist for support, digging her fingers into his jeans, feeling her way to the snap. She unfastened it, then couldn't maneuver the rest. "Wait, wait," she said, breathless from his tongue and teeth doing amazing things to her peaked nipples. He wouldn't listen so she shoved at him until he looked up at her as if she were the most horrible person on earth. "I'm having trouble—you'll have to take them off yourself."

He already had her pants halfway down her thighs, and he stared at the front of her tiny red thong instead of doing as she asked.

Hoping it would get him moving, she got down to panties in record time. He took longer, but only because he had to be careful with his zipper. He made up for it by taking off his boxers along with his jeans. She hurried around to squeeze between the bed and the wall to pull back the covers.

As long as she lived, Cassie would never forget the sight of his aroused body. *Mind-blowing* didn't describe how stunning he was in the raw. Those broad shoulders, a muscular chest that tapered to a flat, slim stomach. His thighs were an athlete's and his erection exceptional. Her gaze swept over him from head to knee and back again. She was used to sevens or eights, and John was an eleven and three-quarters.

With a humph from the opposite side of the bed, John took over the task of yanking off the bedding. Which was good because she was busy.

"Do you have condoms?" she asked, the sudden thought jolting her. "Please tell me you do. Because I don't."

He seemed mildly surprised, then fished two packets out of his wallet. "They're right here," he said, setting them on the thrift-store cherry nightstand. "In case I forget."

"Are you planning on losing your short-term memory?" she asked.

His gaze touched her breasts, then ran down to her thighs, his mouth curving up. "Along with all my other higher functions."

Oh, God. She crawled onto the mattress, absurdly happy that she'd sprung for a top-notch bed. "Why were you surprised I don't have condoms?"

"Was I?"

"Come on."

"I honestly don't remember thinking anything. Short-term memory issues." He kissed her mouth and toyed with the elastic of her panties. "Let's get rid of this."

She'd forgotten about the thong. Before she could take care of it, he moved down to kiss her belly. She tensed, waiting to see where he'd kiss next as he pulled down the red silk. His moist breath bathed the skin at the top of her thighs. Next came his lips, his teeth, the tip of his tongue...until she interrupted to help him draw the panties to her ankles. She used her toes and heel to speed the process. It wasn't fair that she couldn't touch him. She wanted to very badly.

"Come here," she said, then added, "Please," when his slow smile told her he had no intention of hurrying.

"What's the rush?" He dragged the backs of his fingers up the inside of her thigh, and laughed when she clamped her legs together.

She didn't care if he found out she was wet; she simply didn't want it all to end in two minutes. "The reason I don't have condoms," she said, lifting her shoulders off the mattress and curling up until she could almost reach him, "is because I've been too busy for...this..."

"I'm honored you made time for me."

"You should be." She closed her hand around his cock, and the humor left his face.

His strained expression and low moan warned her to be careful or they'd both climax too soon. Leaning back, she stared at the thick hard flesh in her hand. She stroked him, following the upward curve with a light grip that made him pulse against her palm.

"Look who's impatient now," she teased, but payback was swift as he rolled, forcing her to release him, and then hovered over her, using his knee as a wedge between her thighs.

"What was that?" He gave her a sly grin as he stretched out, his leg pinning one of her beneath him.

"Get off, you brute." Her smile undercut her words.

"Brute? Are you kidding? I'm a sweetheart." He didn't wait for her response. Instead, he lifted her chin and took her mouth in a searing kiss that eased into a languid exploration.

Surprisingly, once she'd gotten over the abrupt change, she liked the slow, tense buildup of heat, although sooner rather than later, he'd better start revving things up.

As if he'd read her mind he moved his lips to the base of her throat, planting a kiss at the top of her breast before he sucked a nipple into his mouth. He used just the right amount of pressure and suction to make her quiver, make her want to beg him to ease the burning need inside her. But she wouldn't, not yet.

Gripping his shoulders, she inhaled his scent, clean and as masculine as the muscles that flexed under his warm skin. Try as she might, with him still teasing her breasts, she couldn't reach far enough down to get a grip on his amazing butt.

Balancing himself on his left elbow, he retraced the path on the inside of her thigh until she held her breath, waiting, desperate for him to touch her. She moved her hips against his erection, taking satisfaction in his groan. He lifted his head, and the moment seemed to freeze. He didn't move, just watched her face.

She wasn't sure what was happening, and then gasped at the invasion of his finger sliding into her damp heat. Her shoulders came up off the mattress and she couldn't seem to catch her next breath. He pushed in deeper, and rubbed her with his thumb.

"No," she said. "No. No. No."

He stopped. Everything.

"Oh, God, no, it's just…" She still couldn't seem to catch her breath. "Not yet."

His expression changed in an instant. The intensity returned as his desire flared. He reentered her with two fingers. Found the sensitive nub.

She bucked and clenched, which made everything worse. "You bastard."

"Don't fight it." His heated breath washed over her still-damp nipple. "I'm not going to stop at one." Surging up, he kissed her lips, parted them with his tongue and thrust in rhythm with his fingers.

Eyes shut, Cassie reached for him, but the pressure got to be too much. Everything inside her tightened. She arched against his hand, her body tensing, her breath held. When she came, she bucked so hard it dislodged his fingers. Another spasm hit, not as strong, but more than she expected. He was hot and it had been a while for her, but that didn't explain her body's reaction.

His tongue tracing a line down her torso made her open one eye. He kissed her tummy, then dipped his tongue into her belly button. When he would've slid lower, she grabbed his hair where it was longer on top and lifted his head up. His eyes were dark and hooded, sexier than he had any right to be. "Condom," she said, her voice shaky. "Now."

"Yes, ma'am."

She released his hair, and when he wouldn't move, gave him a shove. "Oh, my God. I've never…"

He kept his slow-eyed gaze on her as he reached for the packet. "You've never what?"

"Come more than once. I just don't."

He returned to his position above her. "We'll have to see about that."

God, he was hard and thick. And hot.

It was his turn to jerk when she rubbed her thumb over the slick tip of his erection. Moving out of her reach, his gaze so dark and piercing she had another after-quake, she watched him slide on the condom.

Her legs spread eagerly and he settled between them with a groan that made her squeeze all the parts of herself she could. She wondered if he were this focused when he strapped himself into his jet, making sure everything was ready for takeoff. The idea was surprisingly sexy.

He rose above her again, leaning on one arm as he guided himself into her, catching and holding her gaze. "Oh, hell, Cassie," he said, teasing her name out low and slow as he pushed inside.

She grabbed the headboard above her head, bracing herself for his entry. He never once looked away from her eyes as he gritted his teeth and drove into her with a powerful thrust that tore a cry from her throat.

Her right hand went to his forearm. With the other she clutched a pillow and wound her legs around his hips. He started to plunge deep, only to pull almost all the way out before doing it again. The pleasure sent waves through her, starting at her center then spreading with the rhythm of oceans, the strength of tides.

Part of her wanted to look down, to roll her head on the pillow, to stop staring, but she was captivated. It didn't stop her from moaning, though, or biting her bottom lip, or calling out when the rogue waves hit.

It was unlike anything that had happened to her before. She never realized that sex had a certain sameness, that she'd come to think of it as a piece, separate from the man she was with, but this...this had everything to do with John.

They were connected. Physically, but way more than that. "Oh," she said, as if that small word could explain it. When she tried for more, it made her blink, so she stopped.

She grew hot in increments. Again, from where he thrust into her, then outward. As if he'd set her blood on fire with a slow match. A prickling sort of heat sparked her nerve endings. God, she didn't know what was happening. It wasn't pressure as much as sheer pleasure that kept building. She wasn't even sure if it was his hand making her feel...

The orgasm overtook her. Her eyes closed.

This was different. Sound muffled, the sheets rubbed against her skin, his weight kept her from floating away, and the tremors, lord, they weren't waves but pounding surf.

Somewhere in the outer world, he stopped and a sound from deep in his throat broke through. It took a long while to come back from wherever she'd gone. Until the world focused again, and she could breathe without gasping.

John held her in his arms. He pressed his lips to hers

and kissed her gently, savoring rather than taking. Making Cassie feel safe. Safer than she'd felt in a long time.

HIS ARM WAS still around her when Cassie opened her eyes, and her cheek was pressed against his lightly haired chest. Something else new for her. She liked having her space, especially in summer when it was warm even with the air on. She also didn't like bringing men home. When it came to John, it seemed she was willing to break all kinds of rules.

They'd both dozed off sometime around 2:00 a.m., which was good. At least for Cassie. She needed the sleep. Her last exam was tomorrow and tonight she had to work. As much as she hated to, she moved her head to see the digital alarm clock. Only five-twenty. She didn't have to kick John out for a few more hours. It wouldn't be easy, but she had little choice if she wanted to get in some serious studying.

He tightened his hold. "How long have you been awake?"

"Just now. I woke you when I looked at the clock, didn't I?"

"Nope." He rubbed her arm, his fingers grazing her bare breast. "I've been lying here for ten minutes trying to decide how cruel it would be to wake you."

"For?"

John laughed and kissed her hair.

"Need I remind you we already used the second condom?" She threw a leg over his, not surprised to find he was getting hard.

"I'm a pretty creative guy." He rolled onto his side

so they were face-to-face and put his other arm around her, too. "Did I tell you how great you were last night?"

Startled, she looked up at him and laughed.

"At the party."

"Oh."

"Because after we got home, you were spectacular."

He kissed the tip of her nose, then briefly kissed her lips before resting his chin on top of her head. She liked that her cheek ended up against his chest again. Loved that she felt the vibration of his deep, contented sigh.

"So, I was wondering. How come you're so tan?"

"All the topics in the world and you come up with why am I so tan?"

"I couldn't help it. That adorably pale butt was mesmerizing."

She raised her head to stare at him. "Because you think it's adorable, and only because of that, I'll tell you. I'm tan from my weekly spa day. I try to fit in a spray tan between my mani-pedi and facial."

The way he looked at her was priceless. "Now who's adorable? Yard work, goofus. I mow the grass and weed in my swimsuit."

"Lucky neighbors."

"Most of them are over seventy. They wouldn't care if I were naked."

"Here I thought you were smart," he said, his face lit with amusement. "You don't have a clue about men."

"The hell you say. I'm around enough of them."

"When it comes to a naked woman, as long as a man is breathing—"

"Stop." She groaned, squeezing her eyes shut. "Thanks

for that— Just what I need, to picture Ed Gibbons from next door leering at me through the blinds…eww."

He captured her hand and only then did she realize she'd been inching toward his cock. "When is yard-work day?"

"Why?" She peeked at him through half-closed eyes. "Do you want to help?"

"Depends. You ever wear a thong bikini?"

Laughing, Cassie tried to twist out of his hold.

He used the distraction to slide down and kiss her breast. He teased her nipple with his teeth and tongue, and she dug her fingers into his shoulder. The rough feel of his stubble against her skin sent pleasure shimmering through her. Already she was damp, and damn it, why didn't she have a box of condoms stashed?

After giving her other breast equal attention, he kissed his way back up to her face. "Any chance you'll be off tonight?"

"None." She finger-combed his hair off his forehead. And smiled when it tumbled back down. "Even if I didn't go in, it wouldn't be so I could play."

"You have to crack the books."

"Yep, but tomorrow is my last exam, which is awe-some. The bad news is that my professor wrote the textbook we used this semester, so I'd better know the material inside and out."

"Can you get off early to study?"

"I'm hoping to, but only if Tommy steps up. I'm not counting on it." She wanted to kick herself for adding the last part. Her brother had his good qualities. She didn't want John thinking he was a total jerk. "I probably haven't made it clear that it's important I have the time off. But I will, and he'll pitch in."

John didn't believe her. She saw the mix of pity and irritation in his eyes. But he left the matter alone. "Is there anything I can do to help? Quiz you? Stimulating massage?"

"Oh, right, that'll work."

"What?" His mouth curved in a guilty smile.

"Don't 'what' me." She ducked her head to rub her cheek against him, mostly to hide her pleased blush. He seemed to really want to see her again. It could've easily gone the other way so she'd tried to not get her hopes up. "Last night…" she said. "You were pretty great yourself."

He hesitated. "At the party?"

"Actually, yes," she said. "Not that you weren't great back here, but I meant at the party…when I told your friends that I'm a bartender."

"What's that?" He nudged her into looking up. "I don't recall saying anything."

She petted his chest. "Didn't you want to explain bartending is temporary, and I'm a grad student?"

"No." He looked puzzled. "Why would I?"

"So they know I don't plan to work behind a bar the rest of my life."

"Why would you care what they think?"

"Not me. You."

John frowned at her, then rolled back to glance at the clock. "I work with those guys. That's it. I don't owe them anything." He faced her again with a smile. "Now, making the best use of our time? That concerns me." He brushed the hair off her cheek. "I figure you'll be throwing me out soon."

"Yes, I will."

"Then we better get busy."

Of all things, Gwen's words popped into Cassie's head. Her insistence that Cassie wasn't wife material. Why would he care what anyone thought when he was only looking for a good time during his leave?

John slid down to kiss her breasts, then just below her rib cage. By the time he got to the top of her thighs, she'd lost her train of thought.

_11_

AT TWO-THIRTY in the afternoon, John started a pot of coffee before he talked himself into going back to bed. He'd had too little sleep, and his room was dark and cool thanks to good blackout shades. Poor Cassie was just as sleep-deprived and had no choice but to study, and then had to show up at the bar in an hour.

It reminded him too much of what it was like for him all during his pilot training. The never-ending cycle of work and schoolwork, and the irrational belief that sleep was for the weak.

He'd left her place around eight, and thought about her the whole way back to his condo. He was really glad that he'd asked her to go to the party, even if his timing was nothing short of rude. She'd been an ace in what could have been an uncomfortable situation. She'd known it, too. Her asking him about the bartending bit told him she truly did understand air force officer culture.

Was that why he'd brought her? To show her off, or worse, as some kind of rebellious statement? It didn't feel as if he'd used her, but he hadn't been himself lately, and he didn't know what that was about, either.

He grabbed his phone from the charger, carried it with him to the living room and sprawled out on the couch while he checked for messages. Much as he didn't expect to hear from her, he was kind of hoping he would. But no, nothing from Cassie. He did have two voice mails, one of them from Mike.

Shit.

Moony rarely called him, which meant he probably wanted to talk about last night. Though everything had seemed cool between them after Cassie walked off with Gwen. And surely Moony didn't blame him for his wife's inappropriate behavior. John hadn't asked her to touch him, and he'd made it clear it was unwelcome.

A whiff of the brewing Columbian drew him back to the kitchen. He filled a mug before he punched in Mike's number, prepared to leave a message since Mike was at work. Luckily, he answered.

"Hey...what's up?"

"I'd wanted to talk to you last night but you left too soon." Mike had to be near the hangar. The fading noise from a Raptor engine drowned out half his voice. "Wait a second...I'm on the move."

John listened to the familiar background sounds, trying to decide if he missed being on the base. There was an odd comfort in hearing a fighter take off and land. But he had to admit, he was enjoying his leave. Primarily because of Cassie.

"I just came off a three-hour debriefing that should've taken two," Mike said when it was quieter. "Goddamn Sanford's got a stick up his ass today."

"He always does." Bullshit debriefings John definitely didn't miss. "So you flew this morning."

"Yeah. Wasn't scheduled to. Good thing Gwen and I left shortly after you and—is it Cassie or Cassidy?"

"Cassie." He wondered if Mike's wife had told him about Cassie's using-him-for-sex comment. Well, yeah, of course she had. John smiled.

"She seems like a real spitfire."

"Oh, she is."

"Gwen really liked her. She was hoping we could all get together for dinner."

Christ. Was that why he'd called? John squeezed the bridge of his nose. "That would be hard. She works nights."

"No problem if you can't. I told Gwen I'd mention it." Mike paused. "By the way, she had one too many margaritas. She didn't mean anything."

"Already forgotten."

Mike quietly cleared his throat. "The reason I called, some of us—Towlie, Rufus and maybe Waldo… We're planning an Alaskan fishing trip. We figured we'd hop a transport to Seattle, rent a plane and then fly to Seward. Book a few one-day charters. My neighbor went last year. He said the halibut and salmon fishing is unreal."

"When?" John wasn't into standing around holding a pole, but he knew that bunch. There'd be more to the trip than fishing. "I don't know when I'll get more leave."

"Not right away. We're in the planning stages."

"How long a trip?"

"Personally, I'd like to go for ten days, minimum. But Gwen would bitch. But then she'll complain even if I take off for a week."

"Ah...come on. You're still newlyweds."

"Screw you, Devil." Mike laughed. "Wait until it's your turn. Let's see how you handle being on a short leash."

"Never happen, buddy."

"Marriage or the short leash?"

His knee-jerk response was to say both. But that wasn't true. "Nothing's slipping around this neck."

"We'll see. Half my damn reenlistment bonus is gone, and I only got the check three months ago." Mike kind of laughed again, but he wasn't fooling anyone. "Hell, I'm not sure where the money all went."

John hoped he was exaggerating. They were talking six figures.

"Don't think I'm complaining about Gwen. I'm not. She likes to look good, and I want her to. It's just—" His sigh was pure frustration. "I figured I'd better grab some of that bonus for the fishing trip. I can't remember the last time we all got together. Been a while."

There was a good reason he couldn't remember. The five of them had never gone out of town as a group. But John knew the chatter was more about steering the conversation away from Mike's wife. "Yeah, sounds good," he said, wondering if he'd still be around. "Let me know once you guys work out the details, and I'll find out if I can get leave."

"You're coming up on reenlistment soon, right?"

John briefly closed his eyes. Why had he thought for one second that it wouldn't come up? "Yep."

"Don't sign until they give you a week off for Alaska."

"Right." John knew everyone assumed he was staying put. And why not? He'd be crazy to give up his air force career. He knew that. Trouble was, it didn't make his decision any easier.

"You got plans for the money?"

"What? I go on leave and everybody slacks off? You have nothing to do but talk on the phone all day?"

Mike told him what he could do to himself, then exhaled into the phone. "That's right, you're still single. You don't have to think one step ahead."

"I'm single, yeah, but I'm not twelve. I'll invest."

"Attaboy, Devil. You always were the brightest of the bunch. Just remember, though…before you buy that diamond ring, choose carefully, my friend. Find a woman who won't embarrass you, makes you look good, but can stand on her own. And make sure you have a secret bank account," Mike said, pretending that last part was a joke.

"I'll keep that in mind." He sure as hell wouldn't marry someone like Gwen. Or any woman who expected him to toe her line, or begrudge him a trip with the guys. But then being with the right woman meant John would rather stay home with her.

"This Cassie…anything serious there?"

"I haven't known her long enough."

"How'd you meet?"

"A bar."

"That's where I met Gwen," Mike said, though he knew that wasn't news to John. "You meet her parents yet? The bikers?"

John didn't like where he thought this might be

headed. "Did you always meet your dates' parents when you were single?"

"Hey, I was just curious. You gotta admit she's not your usual type."

"No." He'd give him that much. But then he had to add, "She's smarter."

"Jesus, don't get defensive. I didn't mean anything. She was interesting, that's all."

"Yes, she is."

"Hey," Mike said, "I gotta get back to work. For the hell of it, mention dinner to Cassie. Maybe the next time she has a free night the four of us can get together."

"Sure," John said. "I'll do that." Naturally he wouldn't. He already knew how she felt about Gwen. What bothered him more at the moment was the implied warning from Mike.

While he appreciated the intent, he didn't like the assumption behind it. Cassie was nothing like Gwen. The two women didn't even belong on the same planet together. He wasn't talking about Gwen's sense of style, either, because whatever made a woman feel like she looked good was fine by him. It was her sense of boundaries that made John uncomfortable. Gwen might be a wonderful wife, someone Mike dearly loved, but she did him no favors.

They disconnected, and John went to the kitchen to get rid of the cold coffee. In a way, he felt sorry for Mike. The other wives and girlfriends didn't seem high on Gwen, either, and John suspected that as a couple they probably weren't invited to more intimate gatherings. Cassie was fresh off the boat. She didn't know Gwen yet and might be willing to get cozy. Or…

John kept circling back to the notion that Mike perceived Cassie as a version of his wife. He obviously didn't know Cassie, so it was nothing to get annoyed over. And what did John care, anyway? He'd never given a damn about what his fellow officers expected of him outside his duties. Of course, he'd always toed the line. Gone out with women who were either one-night flings or bring-home-to-momma material.

Cassie wasn't either one. He certainly wanted more than last night and this morning. But getting serious? Nah, this was a leave thing. That was all.

With a heaviness in his chest, he refilled his mug. He had to admit, though, that when she'd said her parents were bikers…he'd cringed. It had been complete reflex, and he'd covered the gaffe quickly. Lucky for him, Cassie hadn't seen it. But just because he'd gotten away with being a jerk didn't mean he was in the clear. He felt like crap every time the memory flashed.

Maybe it was Gwen's style that made him not like her. Maybe he was a stuck-up pilot who thought he was better than everyone else. He'd have to be deaf, blind and stupid not to see that was the prevailing attitude of his kind.

His kind.

Yes, he led a charmed life, always had, really. But he'd never thought of himself as a snob. Probably because he was up to his eyeballs in snobs just like himself.

Maybe accepting Wagner's offer to be his personal pilot would be a smart move. It would get John into the real world. As soon as the thought sunk in, he caught the error in his thinking. He would only be trading one rarified subculture for another. Tony Wagner was extremely wealthy. The hotels would be five-star, the restaurants, the clubs, the women. John wouldn't suddenly become Joe Everyman.

He sipped his coffee, his thoughts turning to Cassie, and before he knew it, he pulled his phone from his pocket and pressed speed dial. She was either studying or getting ready to go to work. He had no business interrupting, but he wouldn't keep her. Maybe she'd like to know he was thinking about her...maybe he'd stop feeling like crap once he heard her voice.

All he heard was her brief voice-mail message telling him he knew what to do if he wanted his call returned. That was enough to make him smile.

CASSIE PLUNGED HER HANDS into the sudsy water filled with dirty mugs and cursed the broken dishwasher. She cursed again when she realized she'd forgotten to slip on the rubber gloves. That she now gave a rat's ass about keeping her hands soft and smooth warranted another juicy cuss word. But she saved it for Tommy. Assuming he'd ever show up.

The Gold Strike was hopping. A bunch of new people had come in with the hospital gang because it was Beth's birthday. And sucker that she was, Cassie had bought the ingredients to make a piña colada, which Beth had wanted earlier in the week. Now, everyone at her table had ordered one.

"I have a few spare minutes." Lisa set her tray down, then turned to take a final sweep of the room. "Want me to wash, fill pitchers or make the piña coladas?"

"How about going over to Tommy's and dragging

him back here by his ear?" Cassie looked up only briefly. She was so damn angry, but she didn't need to drag Lisa into it. "Actually, I'll settle for you taking care of the pitchers or washing mugs. And thanks."

Lisa slipped behind the bar and stuck a pitcher under the tap. While it filled, she elbowed Cassie aside. "You make the piña coladas. I can wash and watch the pitchers at the same time." Her gaze went to the textbook half hidden by a stack of clean rags. "Oh, and after this round, I'm telling Beth we ran out of colada ingredients."

"You won't be completely lying. I have enough pineapple juice for only one more drink."

The door opened and they both looked over. No Tommy, but more customers. Great.

Cassie sighed. She was tired and unprepared for tomorrow's exam. Part of it was her fault because she should've known better than to let John stay over last night. There wasn't enough discipline in the world that would've allowed her to choose sleep over his clever hands and hard, warm body.

And what had she done after he left? Lazed around, sipping coffee and replaying one of the most amazing nights of her whole life. God, the man was sexy and talented. Funny. Smart. And he'd wanted her…Cassie O'Brien. There was no mistaking how much. Oh, she'd gotten in a couple hours of cramming, and then fell dead asleep on top of her open book. By the time she'd roused herself, she'd had to hightail it to the Gold Strike. Though not after calling Tommy, begging him to open so she could come in later. He'd turned her down, vowed he would if he could but he had an appointment.

She'd explained the importance of tomorrow's exam, and was pleased when he actually seemed sympathetic. She was even happier when he promised to relieve her by seven-thirty. It was now eight-forty, and he wasn't answering his phone. Stupid bastard. There'd been no misunderstanding. She'd been very, very clear. He knew how much she was counting on him, and that was what hurt. Really hurt, like a knife to the heart.

Putting on a smile wasn't easy as she walked to the other end of the bar, where the newcomers had found stools, but it wasn't the customers' fault her brother was a selfish ass.

"Hi. What can I get you, gentlemen?" She didn't know them, but the short guy with the shaggy hair and beard waved at Gordon and his crew sitting in the corner.

"Beer," the younger, taller man said. "Whatever's on tap." He gave her a flirty smile, nothing offensive. In fact he was kind of cute in a yuppie sort of way, which made the pair even odder. Normally she would've smiled back, been more friendly, especially because of their connection to Gordon. But tonight trying not to scowl ate up most of her energy.

"And you?" She waited for the man to stop making hand signs to Gordon as if they were communicating in some juvenile secret code.

He finally turned to her. "What's that, honey?"

"Would you like a drink?"

"Yeah. Let's see…" He played with his beard and frowned at the bottles of booze against the back wall. His gaze jerked to the left, and he grinned. "I'll have me one of those."

She knew without looking that Lisa was pouring the piña colada blend into glasses. Wonderful…this guy who looked as if he drank straight tequila with a side of nails for breakfast wanted a froufrou drink. Just perfect. Tempted as she was to ask if he wanted a miniature umbrella with it, she kept her mouth shut and headed back to her station. He'd likely say yes.

The door opened again, and she prayed with everything she had that it was Tommy.

Even better, it was John.

He looked right at her, and his smile, oh, God, his smile was really something. Not only was he gorgeous in his worn jeans and tan polo shirt molding his biceps and fit torso, but she also knew what was under those clothes. Heaven help her, a blush started somewhere around her chest and surged up her throat to her cheeks.

She quickly turned away, and looked directly into Lisa's amused eyes. Her gaze shot to John, and then came back to rest on Cassie's warm face.

"You little sneak," Lisa said, her grin taking over her features. "When were you going to tell me?"

"Tell you what?" Cassie gave her a puzzled frown, peppered with enough irritation to send a clear message. Then busied herself with getting out the last of the pineapple juice and maraschino cherries.

"Come on…give it up." Lisa sidled up to her, totally ignoring the three drinks Cassie hastily garnished and set on the tray.

"Sure would help if I knew what you're talking about."

"Oh, please. You know what. Your cheeks are redder than those cherries."

"Take these to Beth and her friends, and tell her no more, I'm out."

"Fine. If you won't tell me, I'll ask John." Lisa lifted her chin at the same time she hefted the tray.

"Go ahead." Cassie snorted a laugh. "I'd like to see that."

With a disgruntled huff, Lisa left.

Cassie whipped up another piña colada while she filled two mugs, one for the new guy, one for John. Damn it, how had Lisa known they'd seen each other outside the bar just from looking at him? He'd smiled, that was all. Yes, he might've given her a heart-stopping look at the same time, but... Oh, God, had she been the one to give it away? She'd smiled back, nothing girlie, or sappy, just a plain ordinary smile she gave to every customer.

Or not. Oh, boy.

How could she possibly look at him without remembering his mouth on her breasts? Or how he used the tip of his tongue to make those tiny circles on the soft skin inside her thigh.

Snapping back to the present, she rescued the overflowing mugs, then grabbed a clean rag and wiped the beer off the handles. She picked them up, and made the mistake of looking over to see John watching her with those damn bedroom brown eyes and that ridiculously sexy smile of his. The heat still burned in her cheeks, and before she could think rationally, she gulped down half the ice cold beer from one of the mugs.

Lisa chose that moment to return, and let out a startled laugh. "What are you doing?"

Cassie shook her head, wiped her mouth with a cocktail napkin in case there was foam clinging to her lips and set the beer aside. "I couldn't carry all of them, anyway," she muttered, and picked up the piña colada and full mug.

Keeping her eyes averted, she carried the drinks to the two men. The younger guy was sitting on John's usual stool, so he'd settled on another one closer to the wall. It was more private…if she ever got some time to talk. The men wanted to start a tab, and she tried to not look disappointed. A trio of regulars sat closer to her station, so really, what were a couple more customers sitting at the bar? Maybe she'd take home some decent tips for a change.

She filled out a slip for the newbies, then moved closer to John, but she didn't dare look into his eyes. "Beer?"

He put his elbows on the bar and leaned forward, gazing at her. His lazy smile told Lisa everything she wanted to know. "Hey."

Without her permission, her gaze went to his, and the sounds of the bar faded. Memories flooded her, all of them visceral enough that her next breath trembled. A snort of laughter from the left brought her back as if she'd been slapped. She cleared her throat and threw on a casual smile. "Going once, twice—"

Clearing his own throat, he straightened. "Yes. Please."

Cassie spun around, and damn it, Lisa was waiting for her.

"Wow." The word was out of her mouth before Cassie reached her, and she didn't seem one bit cowed by a glare that should've singed her short hairs. "Wow."

"Don't." Cassie put up her index finger. "Seriously."

It was too late.

Gordon and his half of the room were already staring at her.

12

CASSIE LEANED AGAINST the storage closet door, head pressed against the cool wood. She couldn't remember the last time she'd had a good cry. Not the kind where a couple of blinks made the tears go away. She was thinking more the real deal, like someone had turned on a faucet and no amount of self-recrimination or willpower could stop the flood.

She was seconds away from that cry right now.

This was her first moment alone after making a fool of herself in front of the whole bar. No one, aside from Lisa's few words, had said a thing, but she'd gotten looks from the regulars that made her want to cringe.

This was why she didn't date customers. She was a private person, and being behind the bar had literally and metaphorically given her distance from those she served. Becoming a pseudo Alex Trebek was another layer of protection, and that was how she liked it. And she'd folded like an old paper bag with one look into John's eyes.

It would have been okay if they were something more than a fling, but they weren't and now the word would spread, and life at the Gold Strike would become infinitely messier.

Tommy was still a no-show. She hadn't so much as glanced at her textbook for two hours and she was scared to death she was going to totally screw up her exam tomorrow. She felt self-conscious in her home away from home, and she'd barely looked at John in the past half hour.

It wasn't his fault. Part of it, yeah, because…God… that smile. He'd melted half the ice cubes in the joint. But she was to blame, as well. It hadn't helped that Lisa kept poking for details. And that she'd seen Cassie down half a mug of beer.

Now, all she wanted to do was leave. The lack of sleep combined with her disappointment in Tommy was really getting to her. Five minutes ago she'd decided she was done calling him. She'd already left four messages, and continuing the nonsense was only hurting her. Each time she'd hit speed dial her stomach cramped. At this point, her precious study time wasn't the only thing slipping away. So was her relationship with her brother.

Before, when they were kids, and even in later years, up to and including his tour in Iraq, Tommy would've done anything for her. Anything.

She mourned that closeness they'd once shared. She hated that she couldn't count on him for even simple things. And she very much hated that John knew Tommy had failed her.

Straightening her shoulders, she went back to her post and filled the hell out of Lisa's order. Thank goodness she wouldn't have to use the blender again, but there were far too many people ordering cocktails instead of beer.

"Cassie?"

At the sound of John's voice she met his worried gaze. He motioned for her to join him.

Grabbing a damp rag, she stopped to wipe the bar between him and the other two customers because it was needed, and not as an excuse to go to John. Screw that.

"Hey." She glanced at his mug. He'd barely touched his beer.

"What's going on? You look like you're in a daze."

"I am." She tried to shrug it off with a laugh that fell flat. What was nice, though, was that she felt better being this close to him. Being able to see the details of his handsome face, seeing the concern that lingered in his eyes. Uh, maybe that she could do without. She focused on wiping the counter.

"You get a lot of studying done?" He moved his hand across the bar as if he wanted to touch her, but caught himself.

"I fell asleep. Did a face-plant in my book."

"Oh, Cassie."

She shrugged. "Last night…" Keeping her voice low and throwing a quick glance over her right shoulder, she said, "I wouldn't change anything."

His gaze stayed on her face. "I was selfish. I'm sorry."

"Hey, I just said I wouldn't change a thing."

He smiled a little. "You look beat."

"Yeah, well, I'll probably take a nap when I get home. Just an hour, and I'll be good to go. I'll do a quick review of the material."

"What time is the exam?"

"Nine."

John sighed, then frowned at his watch. "When can you get off?"

Hell, this is what she'd dreaded. "Soon."

"Is Tommy in the back?"

Shaking her head, she looked toward the pool tables. It was crowded back there, too. She knew there were a lot of quarters lined up as folks waited their turns. When she glanced at the group in the front room, she caught Gordon and his cohorts staring at her and John. Her shoulders slumped. She didn't even have the energy to volley a glare.

"Where is he?" John's features had tightened, the tic at his jaw pronounced.

"Don't, okay?" She heard Lisa call for her. "Just don't." She locked gazes with him for a second, hoping he received the message that she really needed him to back off, then she left to fill the latest order.

"What did you say to him? He looks mad." Lisa had come around to wash glasses while Cassie got to work pouring four gin and tonics.

"It's nothing. He just—" She sighed, pausing to sort out how much she wanted to admit. "He knows about my exam tomorrow."

"Tommy still hasn't called?"

Cassie knew better than to attempt constructing a whole sentence. It wasn't so much that she feared every cuss word she knew would likely come out, but that she might burst into tears. Instead she kept her head down, knowing Lisa would get it.

"I wish I could handle the place by myself," Lisa

said, the sympathy in her voice not helping Cassie remain stoic. "Sometimes I can, but not tonight."

"It's okay, really."

"I should pull Lou or Spider from the back. They drink enough, they should know how to bartend."

"No."

"Use me."

Cassie and Lisa looked up at the same instant.

John stood directly in front of them on the other side of the bar. "Let me cover for you, Cassie," he said, the softly spoken words affecting her in startling slow motion.

If she didn't know better she would've sworn he'd touched her. Cupped her cheek, brushed a kiss across her lips, stroked his hand down her back. "What?"

"Please. Let me do this while you study."

Damn him if he was what ended up making her cry. It was bad enough that the customers had seen her go all gooey with John. Crying was out of the question. She was the one who came to other people's rescue. It was always her riding in to make everything right. She never needed anyone's help. She carried the world on her shoulders just fine. Problem was, she couldn't tell him to go away because her voice wouldn't work.

"Your book is right here," Lisa said, and moved the pile of rags. She waited for Cassie to respond, then gave up on her and said to John, "She can study in the storage closet right back here. It's small but big enough, and she has earbuds to block the noise. If you need her she won't be far."

"She won't be disturbed," he said, so convincingly even Cassie believed him.

He came around to their side of the bar, which snapped her out of her trance. "No. You can't do this."

"Why not?" He picked up a clean towel and threw it over his shoulder. "Hey," he said to Lisa, who'd slipped past him to return to the floor. "Will you handle the register?"

"Absolutely."

Damn it, he wasn't listening. Neither of the coconspirators would look at her. Though everyone else in the place seemed to be doing both. She gave a general glare in a sweeping arc, and by then she was able to face John with a good head of steam to steady her.

"John," Cassie said deliberately, "the answer is no. You don't know how to mix drinks."

"Says who?" He glanced around at the occupied tables. "Lots of beer drinkers. So that's easy. As far as cocktails go, tonight everyone's drinking either gin and tonic, tequila sunrises or hard liquor...neat or on the rocks."

"No, they're not." Cassie tried to yank the towel off his shoulder, but he caught her hand. "I've had orders for piña coladas, rusty nails and—"

"From this moment on, those are their choices. Or they can talk me through a drink I don't know. It won't kill anyone." He smiled and squeezed her hand, low, where no one could see. "Most of these guys in here... They're your people, Cassie. If they knew the tough spot you were in, they'd want to help."

"They're paying customers," she muttered.

His strong muscled chest was right there in front of her, only a few inches, and she had the sudden and horrifying desire to bury her face against him. If she moved closer he'd put his arms around her. She knew he would, and she could hide from all her problems. If only for a few minutes.

"Come on," he said gently and picked up the book, holding it out to her. "Get crackin'."

Lisa chuckled. "I like him," she said, then left with her loaded tray.

"You can let me go now." She looked pointedly at the hand engulfed in his, and he released her. When she turned, she saw that Gordon and his crew weren't thrilled about what had just happened. "Some of those guys might give you a hard time."

"I thought we agreed I can take care of myself."

She smiled up at him, ordering herself not to get lost in those warm brown eyes. Not to fool herself into thinking this was anything more than him being a nice person doing a nice thing. "Thanks," she said in a steady voice, then melted a little when he winked.

"THREE GIN AND TONICS, two vodka tonics, tequila rocks and don't forget the lime wedges this time," Lisa said. "Also, two more—never mind. I'll get the pitchers started."

She scooted around to his side and jumped right in, positioning the pitchers under the tap before moving over to the sink and turning on the faucet.

"I don't know how you two keep up," he murmured, careful to keep his voice down. Cassie was holed up behind the door just a few feet away, and she'd already ducked her head out twice in the two hours since he'd been playing bartender.

"Well, Cassie's fast and we've worked together a long

time, but tonight is extrabusy, plus—" She let out a short laugh. "I don't know if I should tell you."

"What?" He concentrated on carefully filling the shot glass, then dumped the gin over the ice in the tumbler. He couldn't free-pour like Cassie did. The liquor cost would go through the roof if he tried that. "Tell me what?"

Lisa watched him pour the next shot, clearly trying not to laugh. "This isn't brain surgery. Don't be so precise."

"Yeah, well, it's going to be my head Cassie bites off if I mess up her profits."

"Don't worry. Cassie is more generous when she pours. The customers are used to stronger drinks. I'm surprised they haven't complained. Though they've been distracted..." She cursed when she saw the pitchers overflowing and hurried to turn off the tap.

"Okay, here are the gin and tonics." He stood back. "Oh, shit, wait." The lime wedges. Where the hell had he put them?

He groaned when he remembered he didn't have any more cut up. He was supposed to take care of those kind of things in his spare time. Right. As if he'd had a single extra minute. His mouth was dry, and he was so thirsty he'd drink jet fuel at this point.

The door creaked open to the left behind them... Cassie, of course. "Do you need—?"

"No," John and Lisa said at the same time.

"Fine." She shut the door rather loudly.

They exchanged grins, then Lisa said, "Our problem child."

"Third time now. I hope she's gotten the hint."

"Um, you don't know Cassie."

No, he didn't. Not as much as he'd like. At what point he'd arrived at that conclusion he wasn't sure, but he'd seen red when he found out Tommy was in the wind when he knew his sister needed him. He got out the bag of limes and cutting board. Had no idea where he'd put the knife.

Lisa seemed to pull it out of thin air, then waved him away when he reached for it. "Make the vodka tonics. I'll cut up enough for these drinks, deliver them, then come back and finish."

He envied how fast she worked. "Thanks for helping me out."

"Hey, you're the one helping. Cassie deserves this. She deserves you." Lisa paused, frowned, sent him a sidelong look. "Someone like you. Hell, you know what I mean."

John let the comment go and uncapped the vodka bottle. "So, would you say a shot and a half would be about right?"

"Jesus, flyboy, just pour." Laughing, she picked up her tray, balancing the two heavy pitchers and drinks in one hand. "Be right back."

A woman of her word, Lisa used the next lull to cut up limes. He figured he'd hit the bonus round when she started washing glasses. "You're good for business," she said, glancing over at him with a sly smile.

"Okay, I'll bite. How so?"

"You asked earlier how we keep up. We get slammed sometimes at the end of the month and the middle...you know, around payday. Nothing Cassie and I can't handle. But tonight, everyone's ordering extra. They're trying to keep you humping, see how long it takes for you to blow a fuse. And then there's a few who just want to annoy the crap out of you."

"Gee, let me guess who." Gordon, who hadn't liked him from the first, gave him a small nod. John held back his grin, even though he'd take that gesture for the compliment it was.

Lisa followed his gaze. "He knows you're doing this for Cassie. That's major points right there."

A giant bear of a man with an impressive beard and endless tats had come from the pool tables and slammed an empty pitcher on the bar hard. "No wonder service is so shitty. You two standing here gabbing like old ladies. What the hell do I have to do to get a refill around here?"

John had been ready to suck it up and apologize, when Lisa said, "Try shutting up for starters."

Customers at the tables laughed. So did the big guy.

"Damn it, Spider." Lisa grabbed the pitcher and inspected it. "You could've broken this."

"Where's Cassie?" Spider asked, frowning at John. "She's prettier than you." With beefy hands, he gripped the edge of the bar, arms wide, his round belly pressed against the wood while he studied John's face. "Though not by much."

That got another round of laughter.

"Funny. I didn't know it was open-mic night."

John heard the storage closet door open, and turned to see Cassie peeking out. "Everything's fine," he said.

"What was that loud noise?" She saw Spider and rolled her eyes. "Was that you causing trouble?"

"Cassie."

At John's stern tone, she sighed and closed the door.

"Before you get in his face," Lisa said, drawing the man's angry glare away from John, "you should know he's doing this for Cassie. She's back there studying for an exam. Your buddy was supposed to be working this shift."

"Where is he?"

"Who knows?" She set the filled pitcher in front of him. "He won't answer Cassie's calls."

Spider's brows furrowed and his irritation with Tommy seemed legit. He went back to sizing up John, the mischievous gleam entering his eyes hard to miss. "Our girl is more than a bartender. She knows her stuff," Spider said. "Dude, you got some big shoes to fill."

John snorted a laugh. "You going anywhere with this?"

"See you, boys." Lisa picked up her tray, and as she slipped to the other side of the bar, she whispered to John, "His bark's worse than his bite."

Spider picked up the pitcher and drank from it as if it were a mug. He wiped the foam off his beard with the back of his arm. "Where's the cheapest gas in town? You got five seconds."

John folded his arms across his chest. "The Pilot on Craig."

Rearing his head back, Spider eyed him with suspicion for a moment, then said, "No shit?"

"Nah. That's what I heard Cassie tell someone the other day. For all I know they could've doubled the price by now."

Several customers thought that was pretty funny. So did Spider. "You're all right, pretty boy, you're all right," he said, nodding, and then took his pitcher with him back to his pool game.

A guy sitting at Gordon's table yelled, "Hey, bar-keep…"

John looked over, saw everyone's grins and waited for the smart-ass question he figured was coming.

"The Cheyenne exit is closed for construction. What's the quickest detour to get downtown?"

"I know this one." While he answered, he took up where Lisa had left off, washing glasses and mugs, and letting them dry on the rack.

For the next hour, different customers shot out random questions. He replied truthfully to the ones he knew, responded to the absurd queries with the silly answers they deserved. It was all in fun and made the time fly. Lisa had clued him in on the betting pool the regulars had started the minute he'd taken over for Cassie. Evidently him lasting twenty minutes was the long-shot wager.

Since he'd disappointed them, they'd started a new pool. Now they were betting on how long it would take him to break down and call Cassie for help. Fine with him. They were ordering drinks by the case. He just hoped they tipped Lisa and Cassie accordingly.

"I have a question."

John glanced up from cutting limes and into the flushed face of a short blonde. If she'd been sitting with one of the groups, he hadn't noticed her. She looked young, and he wondered if he should card her. "Yes?"

"I'd prefer to talk to Cassie," she said, her voice lowering.

Ah, he got it now. Someone was hedging their bet. "She's not available."

"It's kinda important."

"Sorry, it's me or nothing."

"What about Lisa? Where is she?"

"Taking a smoke break. She'll be back in ten minutes."

"Oooh." She seemed genuinely distressed, biting at her lip, her cheeks growing pinker. But he wasn't fooled by her act. "It'll only take a few seconds."

"I'm not calling Cassie out here, so if you really need something, I suggest you spit it out."

She took a deep breath. "The machine in the ladies' room is broken. I need a tampon."

John blinked, stared at the woman for a moment, then looked over his shoulder. "Hey, Cassie."

Everyone, without exception, laughed. Even the bald guy who dug in his pocket and had the twenty promptly plucked from his fingers. A side bet, obviously.

"You're good," he told the grinning blonde, who then turned and bowed to her audience.

Behind him, he heard the storage door creak…at the exact moment the front door opened.

It was Tommy.

A little unsteady, he looked as if he were drunk. Or barely awake. He stopped just inside, panning the room, his smile growing with the infectious laughter. When his gaze came to John, all humor left Tommy's face. "Get the fuck out from behind my bar."

13

ALERTED BY THE SUDDEN silence after laughter that had made her grin, Cassie dropped her pen as the words came through the door.

Her entire chest felt as if it had imploded. Her fury at Tommy was only equaled by her concern. The last thing anyone needed was a fistfight in the middle of the bar. But knowing her brother and his hair-trigger temper, it could happen.

She was off her chair in an instant, barely noticing her book fall to the floor. Once the door opened, it was like staring into a nightmare.

"I'm helping Cassie," John said, his voice low and serious. She could hear the razor-thin restraint. "She's in back. Studying."

Before Tommy could respond, she stepped out, keeping her distance from John. The situation was too volatile and her goal was to stop things right now. The bar was packed, and Tommy... One look at him told her he'd been drinking. God, she wanted to strangle him. But later. "I'm right here," she said. "Everything's fine.

Thank you, John, for lending a hand, but we've got it covered now."

His shoulder muscles flinched, as did his jaw, but he never took his eyes off Tommy. John's arms were loose at his sides, his body ready for anything.

Tommy wasn't nearly so grounded. His rage made his face a dull, dangerous red. He'd worn his prosthesis, but everything about him was unsteady. Fisted hands were halfway raised, and she could tell he was working himself up. "You goddamned officers think you can do anything you please. Walk into a man's bar and take over. Thinking you're better 'an me, better 'an all of us. What the hell are you doing in here anyway? Slumming? I saw that Corvette of yours. Too good to park in the lot, huh? Don't want anyone mistaking you for one of us. God forbid someone thinks you're enlisted."

"Tommy," Cassie said, as strongly as she'd ever said anything in her life. "Stop it. Now."

"You think you can get into my sister's pants by helping her at the bar? You think she's stupid? You're so obvious it's pathetic. Well, I've got news for you. She wouldn't look at you if you were the last man on earth."

"That's it," John said, tossing the towel from his shoulder to the bar. "You want to know what I'm doing here? Picking up your slack, that's what. You knew Cassie needed to study, but you couldn't be bothered to come in to your own goddamn bar and give her a break. I'm doing what you should have had the decency to do. She's got one more test, one more. And you couldn't even return her phone calls."

Tommy took a step toward the bar and almost lost

his balance, but two of the regulars jumped to grab him. "Let me go," he said, his voice quavering with anger.

The men didn't. Thank God. Cassie took her own step closer to John. She touched him, low, her hand covered by the bar. "Please," she said, keeping her voice down. "Please, just go."

"Get off me," Tommy shouted. "You happy now, Cassie? Now you've turned my friends against me?"

"John. I can't do this. You need to go. I'll be fine."

When he looked at her, the struggle was so clear, she wanted to comfort him, but this wasn't the time. Tommy had to calm down. He could seriously hurt himself or someone else. He'd already humiliated himself to the point where it made her sick.

She took hold of John's hand and squeezed it as she walked him to the end of the bar, letting go as soon as it would have been seen. But she continued on with him until he was at the front door. "Thank you," she said, as softly as she could. She didn't touch him at all, but she prayed he understood that she wanted to. Badly. "We'll talk later. I appreciate everything you've done."

Tommy started ranting behind her, and John looked over, ready to charge in, but she put a hand on his chest. His heart was beating so fast it echoed her own. "Please."

He sighed. Nodded once. Then walked away.

Cassie forced herself to face her brother. It wasn't easy. She loved him, she did, but this was...

He stared at her as if she'd betrayed everything he'd ever held dear. As if she were responsible for all the bad things that had happened to him.

He closed his eyes and jerked himself out of the grip

of Wayne and Greg. When he turned his back on her, he teetered. Greg went to help, but Tommy slapped his arm away. To utter silence, her brother walked between tables, away from her. He didn't move his head, and what was worse, the folks sitting down, longtime regulars and newcomers alike, avoided looking at him.

Her heart felt as if it were breaking into tiny pieces. Maybe it was all her fault. She treated him like an invalid, and that was what he'd become. If she'd been stronger...

"Come on," Lisa said, making Cassie jump. "Let's get back to work. We have orders to fill."

With as much dignity as she could muster, she followed Lisa, making an effort to meet people's eyes, to smile, even though she had to blink back tears.

Once she was by the sink, she picked up the towel John had thrown. It killed her that Tommy had gone to the pool room. The old Tommy would have set aside his pride and taken care of business. Not even considering that he'd ignored her, he shouldn't have turned his back on the bar or his customers.

The anger she'd felt for days, hell, for weeks, came surging up again, but she tamped it down as she looked at the first person who caught her attention. "Need a refill on that gin and tonic?"

It was as if she'd pressed the start button. Bless them, the bikers, the mechanics, the folks from the hospital, all the people who'd become more than customers, started talking. Loudly. Filling the room with sound helped, and for once she was grateful that one of the boys fed a handful of quarters to the jukebox.

"Hey. You." Lisa popped up again. Right next to her.

"Quit doing that."

"I really didn't bring you back here to work. Go get your damn textbook and get out of here."

"I can't."

"Yes," Lisa said, folding her arms over her chest. "You can. And you will. Tommy brought this on himself. He's gonna have to figure a way out of it. By himself."

Cassie opened her mouth to protest, but Lisa's eyes were like flint.

"He needs to fix this, Cass. Go home. Study. And when you see that man of yours, you give him a big sloppy kiss for me. I swear," she said, swiping her forehead with the back of her hand, "I nearly swooned when he stood up for you like that."

"I could have handled it," Cassie said.

Lisa's mouth dropped open a bit. "You stubborn... Yeah, you could have. The point is, you didn't have to. Because you had someone on your side for a change."

"It's not like that—"

"I give up on the both of you. Go home, Cassie. I've got the bar, and if I have to kick your brother's butt all the way across the building, I will."

Cassie didn't doubt her. About Tommy. What she'd said about John? That, she'd have to think about.

JOHN CHECKED HIS WATCH again, wishing he'd brought something to drink with him. He shifted on the step that led up to Cassie's front door, waiting as the warm night ticked away.

She'd probably stay at the bar to finish out the shift. Tommy was too drunk to work, and besides, after that display, the idiot had probably walked out. Leaving his sister to hold down the fort. Again.

John's anger rose once more, as it had ever since he'd honored Cassie's wishes and taken his leave. It had been incredibly difficult. He wasn't in the habit of walking out on such an unstable scene, and especially abandoning the woman he'd come to like so much.

John got to his feet and started pacing. Again. He didn't care if she did stay till closing, he wasn't going anywhere until he saw for himself that Cassie was doing okay. And he needed to tell her that he was sorry. He should have left the first time she asked him to.

She'd done what was necessary for the bar and for herself. She'd even done him a favor. Getting into a physical altercation with her brother would have cost everyone.

He'd known right away that Cassie was smart. She reminded him of the best pilots. Steady as a rock, aware of all the contingencies and she didn't get thrown by surprises. He smiled thinking about her at the party. Maybe she hadn't been dressed like the officers' wives he'd grown used to, but she'd been classy as hell in her own way.

Besides, who said things had to stay the same? Maybe during his mother's generation, the officers' wives were expected to dress a certain way, be willing to socialize with the right people at a moment's notice. But now, his friends' wives were far more independent. Although, they all kind of hung around with each other, didn't they?

But the basic principal was to maintain a level of conduct that honored the fundamental values of serving one's country. He had no argument with that. The fact that he was an officer of the U.S. Air Force was never far from his mind, even when he was waffling about his future. He'd be proud to take Cassie to any event. In fact, he'd like to see her all dressed up. She'd be a knockout.

A car came down the street, the first one in a while, but it wasn't Cassie's old clunker. John sat down on the step again, checked the time. He could call her, just check in, but that might not be the best move. She could be having it out with Tommy, and he wouldn't want to intrude.

On the other hand, maybe she needed a distraction, an excuse to leave? If for nothing else, her studies. Even if she'd been hitting the books since the moment he'd left, the emotional hangover from that scene was going to play havoc with her retention. He knew.

After Danny had died, he'd been a wreck. So had Sam. They'd done their jobs because they'd been trained to the nth degree, but neither one of them had slept worth a damn for months. Getting behind the stick again had been painful. Muscle memory and hundreds of hours of repetition had kept them on course. It was downtime that had sent them spinning.

He and Sam had talked about it. As much as they could, but neither one of them were particularly good at verbalizing their feelings or whatever.

Anyway, he knew Cassie wasn't going to sail through her test. Maybe, if she came home anytime soon, he could—

Another car. This one needed some muffler work.

He stood, and sure enough, there couldn't be another Ford like that on this block.

He ran his hands down his jeans and waited until she pulled into the drive. She must have seen his car before she'd seen him standing on the front step.

She turned off the car, and the engine got the message after she was halfway to him. "What are you doing here?"

"Waiting to make sure you're okay."

"I'm fine." She slowly made her way to his side, her key in her left hand, her books in her right and her purse over her shoulder. He slipped the books from her grip. "Honest. I'm fine. I'm sorry about what happened. He had too much to drink and—"

"Hey, I'm the one that owes you an apology. I should have kept my big mouth shut."

She looked up at him as if to respond, then just shook her head and opened the door.

"May I come in?" he asked, waiting until she'd crossed the threshold.

She winced. "Sure, I guess. But—"

"You know what? I'm sorry to say this, but I only want to talk. We'll be having none of that sexy business."

"None?"

"Maybe a kiss. But that's where I draw the line. Even if you beg me."

She laughed, and it made everything a whole lot better. Not fixed, though. He'd meant it about needing to apologize.

But he let it alone while she turned on more lights

and put down her things. She looked tired, as he knew she would. "What can I get you to drink?" he asked.

"What, an hour behind the bar and now you're a mixologist?"

He shook his head. "I had no idea how difficult your job is. I could barely keep up, even with Lisa's help. I'll tip better from now on."

"I've seen your tips. You don't have a lot of room for improvement."

"Those were special."

"I should hope so," she said, walking toward him, looking very purposeful. "How about you kiss me, then I go visit the ladies' room while you fix us both a cold soda."

"I can do that," he said, pulling her close, pressing her body against his own. She felt amazing, and he breathed her in like the first hit of fresh air after the oxygen mask came off. When he kissed her, she slipped her arms around his neck as he circled her waist.

They started off just brushing their lips together, and when that about drove him crazy, he broached her with his tongue. She tasted like limes, and that made him grin. Not that he quit kissing her, because he might not get another chance tonight.

Running his hand up her back, he could feel the tension in her shoulders, and as badly as he wanted to use all his time to make out, this wasn't about him. He pulled away, glad to hear her little protest, but not giving in to her tug on his shirt. "Go. I'll get the sodas. You have a preference?"

She shook her head.

"Okay, then. See you in a few minutes."

He turned, but was stopped midway. "Thank you. For helping me tend bar. For being patient. For... Well, just thank you."

With a heavy sigh, he reversed so he could look her in the eyes. "I should have made the situation better, not worse."

"You were great. Seriously. And now I'm asking pretty please if we can drop the subject. I've got so much to do tonight, and I'm already whipped."

"You bet. I think I can help with those shoulders of yours. And quizzes. If you need a quiz, I am definitely your man."

Her smile lit up her eyes. Not the way they did when she was rested and hadn't had a major blowout with her brother, but still, he was pleased to see it. "I'll think better after I wash my face," she said, and then she was off.

He chose a cola for her, and a ginger ale for himself. The cracking of the ice made him thirstier still, and he'd downed a considerable amount by the time Cassie came back.

Little fringes of hair around her face were wet. She did seem somewhat more alert as she lifted her soda. "Here's to caffeine and memorization."

He urged her to the couch, where she handed him the textbook open to a list of study questions. It took them several minutes to arrange themselves so that he could massage her shoulders while she answered his questions. As the night went on, her answers came less quickly and were interspersed with yawns.

When the worst of the knots had been teased out of her muscles, he sat beside her. Twenty minutes past midnight, her body rested fully against him, her head on his shoulder.

"Why don't we wrap this up?" he asked. "You can barely keep your eyes open."

"I don't need to see when you're asking the questions. Keep going."

He obeyed, knowing her determination wasn't going to win over her exhaustion.

Finally, she didn't answer a question. He was loath to move her. Not only did she look impossibly young and beautiful, but there was also a certain privilege that came along with her trust. He'd wanted to protect her at the bar, wanted to care for her now. She'd have objected. And it was true, she could take care of herself. Still...

He moved very carefully, slowly, arranging her on the couch until he could stand. A quick trip to her bedroom let him throw back the covers.

Once he returned to the living room, he didn't pick her up immediately. Some urge he didn't linger over had him crouching beside her, pushing back the wisps of now-dried hair. Touching her with his fingertips as he watched her sleep.

As far as distractions went, Cassie had exceeded his expectations. He'd thought of her as an attractive novelty. Perfect for ten days of something different.

That wasn't the half of it. She'd surprised him many times. He'd found her very pretty when he'd first seen her, but now that he knew her, she was gorgeous. There were all her smiles, some still not catalogued. He liked to think understanding her body language was his homework. He didn't mind studying one bit. He wanted to know her by heart before he went back to work.

Of course, the bad part about being so caught up in Cassie's life was that he still had decisions to make about his own.

He stood again, and she stirred when he lifted her, but even in her groggy state she managed to snuggle against his chest and hold on with an arm around his neck. "What time is it?"

He smiled at the slur of her words. "Bedtime."

She sighed and rubbed her cheek against his chest. "'Kay."

By the time he turned out the lights, he'd made sure her alarm was set for seven-thirty, that they were both shoeless, although still dressed, and that he would be there in the morning to make sure she made it to her class on time.

14

"WHERE ARE YOU?" Cassie asked, clutching her cell phone, looking down the street to her left for his Corvette. It was past noon and she'd just finished writing her exam. John hadn't said he'd be picking her up, but she'd bet the farm he was somewhere nearby.

"You're cold."

She straightened, her gaze going across the street.

"Warmer."

Smiling, she turned to her right, and there he was, looking like a star on a sexy car billboard, one hand in his pocket, one up to his ear and his legs crossed as he leaned against the driver's door. "How long did you work on that pose, pretty boy?"

"Um, what time did I drop you off?"

She laughed. "Come on. I'm starving. One piece of toast does not a breakfast make. You need to buy me lunch. I'm thinking deli."

She watched as he climbed inside the car, but she couldn't hear the engine turn over. "Hold on. I'm putting you on the speaker."

He didn't talk again until he'd merged into traffic. "For takeout, yes?"

"What? Oh, I hadn't thought—"

"From the tone of your voice, I'm guessing you did well on the test. Am I right?"

He pulled up in front of her, blatantly ignoring that it was a red zone. She hurried around to the door and slid inside before they got a ticket. "You are," she said, and heard her voice echo. She hung up. "You are," she repeated. "I did well, but even more important, I don't have to study again. At least for a while. I'm a woman of leisure. Except for working seven days a week, and finally giving my house the cleaning I've been putting off for months, and then painting my front door, because it looks like hell."

"Other than that, huh?" he said, pulling into traffic. He was grinning, but then so was she.

"We don't have to do deli if you want something else."

"I don't care about the food. I just want dessert." His hand went to her thigh and snuck under the hem of the sundress she'd worn. "It wasn't easy sleeping next to you last night."

"I appreciate the tremendous sacrifice you made," she said. "Seriously, I called the papers. They're running a tribute on page two."

"Page two?"

She shrugged. "Idiots."

"Deli is fine. We can eat half a sandwich right away, and then the other half after."

Cassie laughed, but slapped at his hand. "You're tak-

ing a lot for granted there, flyboy. Besides, how come
we always end up going to my place?"

"It's nicer."

"Why do I doubt that? Don't tell me you're hiding
a wife and kids in some big old house in Summerlin."

The look he gave her was so outrageous she had to
laugh, although when he didn't outright deny it, her
stomach got a little funny. Which was ridiculous. "No,
really. Why don't we go to your place?"

"Okay," he said. "You'll see, though. Now, where is
that deli again?"

THEY GOT TO HIS PLACE an hour later. When he opened the
door, she was immediately caught by the view. It was
spectacular. Or would be at night with the whole of the
Strip glittering like a diamond runway. Then the white
walls hit her. The nothing. No pictures, no plants, no
books, no mementos from his travels. He put his keys
in his pocket.

"See? Not very homey."

"You didn't strike me as being a neat freak."

"I have someone come in to clean."

"To clean what? Do you have a closet filled to the
brim somewhere in the back?"

"Nope. But I do have an ice machine, and a table.
We can have that half a sandwich now."

"Good. I'm famished." She put the bag from the res-
taurant on the table and started unpacking. There wasn't
much. A couple of Dr. Brown's sodas, two huge sand-
wiches and a few dill pickles.

John filled glasses with ice and came to sit across
from her. "It's not that I'm neat," he said. "I'm just never

here. When I'm not on leave, I work twelve- to fourteen-hour days. That's not even counting when I'm deployed. I can be gone six months at a time."

"But you have a housekeeper," she said, carefully spreading her packet of mustard on her rye. "Although I'm not sure what she'd have to do besides dust. I mean, you don't even have mail on the counter. That's unnatural."

He shrugged as he took an enormous bite. She, on the other hand, had to put half the meat from her sandwich on the wax paper it had come in. After a minute, he said, "I don't have mail because most of it goes to my sister. She pays the bills from a joint account I set up. It's easier when I'm out of the country."

Cassie shook her head. "I swear. What is it about brothers who refuse to grow up?" Then she took her own bite and moaned at the still-warm pastrami. When she looked at John, expecting to find him devouring more of his food, she found him frowning at her instead. She waved her hand at him until she could tell him, "I was kidding. Sheesh."

"I know," he said, without an ounce of conviction. "The way you work and go to school, I don't see how you can have so many things. I mean, I get art, I'm not a complete cretin, but the plants. The goldfish. Those take work, and you've got dozens."

"Only two goldfish. In one bowl."

He rolled his eyes, moving in on a pickle.

"I like having living things around me," she said. "I breathe deeper, walking into a room full of plants. And I love being able to look at pictures or souvenirs that remind me of wonderful memories. I think, if anyone ever cared to, they could put together a very accurate portrait of my life from all the clues I've left. That means a lot to me."

He tipped his head, chewing away, as if telling her he got her point, even if he didn't share the sentiment. "We moved around so much that I never really took to the notion of nesting. My mom made an effort. We had a lot of company, so she wanted things to look nice. All you'd have been able to read back then was that we were an air force family down to the bone. And then, within a year or two, we had to pack all the crap she'd put on the walls, and fill in all the holes left from the nails, repaint. It was a pain in the ass."

"Okay," Cassie said. "I get that. But we never had a home, either. Not like most people. We traveled with the weather. Stayed at campsites, motels, friends' houses. I've been in Vegas longer than any other place. I'd like to get a job here, stay. Especially because of the bar. Tommy can be a complete jerk, but he's mine. And I love him. That being said, I'll go where the work sends me."

John put down his sandwich without taking the last bite. His gaze was pointed toward her, but he wasn't seeing her. Cassie's chest tightened, she had no idea why.

"In nine days, I have to decide whether I'm going to sign up for another tour."

She started to tease him about the obviousness of the answer but it sunk in, what he'd really said. He hadn't made up his mind. Which made no sense. He was a fighter pilot. A profession way up there in the dream-job list. Although…he never talked about flying. At all.

He barely wanted her to know what he did. Huh. "What don't you like about the job?"

He winced. It didn't last more than a second. "Nothing. I love to fly. There's nowhere I'd rather be than in the cockpit."

"What about when you're not in the cockpit?"

"I've got another job offer. Flying a private jet. Loads more money. By a wide margin. A chance to fly to places I've never been. No more debriefings and being sent to war zones. And the plane, damn, it's a G650, which is the finest jet on the market. Tony Wagner, the guy that's offering me the job, is worried I won't want to leave the fighter jets. He really wants me to work for him, so…"

"How did you know him?"

John focused on his food but as he did so, the tips of his ears got a little pink. "I sort of saved his life."

"Sort of?"

"Nothing all that spectacular. One night he was coming out of Caesar's Palace at the same time I was. I didn't know him at all, but we were kind of crowded together by all the tourists. He was pushed onto Las Vegas Boulevard and a car was heading straight for him. I pulled him out of harm's way. Anyone would have done the same, but he was very grateful and we ended up having a drink together."

"I doubt just anyone could have saved him. Your reflexes, your strength. I'm sure he was awfully grateful…" She looked around his empty nest. "So it's the money that's making you think twice about leaving the air force? The perks?"

He shook his head. "Those would be nice, but I'm

doing fine moneywise. I've invested well, and except for ridiculous cars, I don't spend a lot."

"You just want to be a civilian?" The way his brows furrowed, as if she'd said something crazy, made her curious. Surely, with the decision having to be made so soon, he'd thought this through. Growing up the way he had, becoming a civilian at this point would be a major deal. "Wow, I guess being in the bubble has its merits, but in the end, you're still in a bubble."

"What does that mean?"

She shrugged. "Being a fighter pilot and all. You live in a rarified atmosphere even when you're not in the air. It's glamorous and dangerous and very, very alpha. Flying as a private pilot is a whole different kettle of fish, but maybe that's the challenge you're looking for."

"It's not—" He stood up, walked away from the table. From her. The set of his shoulders, the way he paced, he looked agitated, and she wanted to call back her words, even though she wasn't sure what she'd said wrong.

"I do live a charmed life. I know that. I'm the luckiest son of a bitch in the world. I have no business even thinking about leaving the air force. Christ. My friends Danny and Sam would kill to be in my shoes."

He stopped at the window, stared straight ahead.

Cassie ate quietly, watching him. Wondering what was really going on. She was tempted to say something but afraid to interrupt his thoughts. It took a long time for him to turn back to the room.

"We met in college, went through basic together and all the requirements necessary to be allowed to fly the fast movers. The three of us wanted to make it so badly we'd have done anything. Anything. And we did. We all made it through some of the hardest training in the world, and we had our wings and our jets, and it was the best. You can't even…"

"What happened?" She'd lowered her voice, kept it neutral.

"Sam got laser eye surgery so he wouldn't have to wear contacts anymore, but it went wrong. They can't correct his left eye to flight standards. That's it. He's out of the jets. Now he's going to train drone pilots."

"That's got to be horrible for him."

"You have no idea."

"And Danny?"

The answer didn't come quickly. "Dead. In a stupid accident. Not his fault. He was a great pilot. Full of potential. Had life by the balls. A freak mechanical problem and he was gone. Just like that."

"Oh, God, John. I'm so sorry."

"And here I am, feeling *discontent*."

Cassie's breath caught at the disgust she heard in his voice. "But…you're grieving. For your friends. For the dreams you all shared. Of course you're questioning your life."

JOHN STARED AT CASSIE, resisting the urge to discount the facile pop psychology she'd spouted. He knew she meant well. But she was steeped in her Dr. Phil textbooks, where everything could be solved with a good cry. He knew better.

He'd grieved a hell of a long time for Danny. But he'd pulled his shit together when it was time to go back and do the job. As for Sam, he'd made the best of his situation and John was taking his cue from that.

John's hesitation in reenlisting was about where and how he wanted to spend the next ten years of his life. Surrounded by all the people he'd seen for the past ten? Doing what he'd always done because it was expected of him? If he hadn't been born to his family, would he have made the same choices?

Cassie couldn't understand that, not given where she was in her life. She hadn't even reached her primary goals yet. He appreciated that she cared, though. The way he'd cared about her studying last night. They might just be together for a laugh, but she was great, and he wouldn't want to see her hurt. He was sure she felt the same.

He went back to the table, sorry he'd even brought the subject up. He liked it better when they were talking like friends. Or spending some quality time in other pursuits. "You almost done with that?" he asked, nodding at the remains of her lunch.

Her lips parted as if she were about to say something, but it was too tempting a sight for him to pass up. He swooped in for a kiss. The position, him bending low over her chair, was uncomfortable, though, and besides, he wanted more. "I think we need to move this to the bedroom."

"I, uh…"

"We're celebrating," he whispered, his mouth a scant inch from hers, which allowed him to kiss the hesitation right out of her. "We'll need the rest of the food later. Come with me, Cassie. Let's make some fireworks together."

She stood, moving around the chair until she was in

his arms. He went to kiss her, but she leaned her head back. "You sure you're okay?"

"Absolutely. One hundred percent."

Her smile didn't reach her eyes until he brushed the back of his hand over her cheek.

"I mean it. I just want to be with you. The bedroom doesn't have any plants, but the bed's great."

"I'm sure it is."

He kissed her again. Gently at first, letting the steam build. He'd changed gears pretty abruptly and she needed time to adjust. He knew how much she liked it when he ran his hands down to her behind and pulled her close as he teased her mouth.

Slowing things to a simmer, he had no complaints about a leisurely journey to full throttle. Each step had its own merits. One thing he'd learned in the service was patience. He'd give her all the time in the world. He wanted her begging for release, trembling under his tongue. By the time he was done with her, they'd both be too wasted to care about anything but gaining their strength back.

"I have to go to work at five, remember?" she said.

"What? Today?"

Cassie nodded. "Life is full of trials and sacrifice."

He let go of her long enough to lead her down the hall to the master bedroom. The first order of business was to pull down the bedding. Then he turned back to beautiful Cassie, glad she'd been too busy looking at his furniture to start undressing. He wanted to do that.

"It's nice," she said. "Very sleek."

"My sister helped me pick it out. She's good with that sort of thing."

"Ah. But is it your taste?"

He checked over the dark mahogany sleigh bed, the matching bedside tables, the dresser. "Yeah, I suppose. Honestly, the only thing I was picky about was the mattress."

"Well, lucky me," she said, taking her dress in her hands, ready to lift.

He was at her side in a second. "No, no, no. That's my job. Have I mentioned how much I like this dress?"

She shook her head.

"Well, I do." His fingertips went to her shoulders. So close to bare, and yet those two delicate straps were all that stood between him and seeing those pert little breasts. Tasting them, making those nipples bud. For him.

He slipped one finger under each strap. "It must have been so hard for the guys in your class to take that test. One look at you in your sundress and they were done for. I could barely drive home, wanting to watch you. Waiting for the hem to climb up those gorgeous thighs. Picturing what lay beneath."

Pulling the straps over her shoulders, he wondered if the dress would simply fall. No, sadly. The bodice was just snug enough that it would take a bit of effort on his part.

"My goodness," she said, her voice throaty and low. "What's gotten into you, Captain Devil?"

"Uh-uh. Backward. It's the thought of me, getting into you, that has me like this." He steadied her with one hand as he let her feel how hard he was. It had happened so fast, from zero to flight speed. The dress, it had to be the sexy dress.

"That must be uncomfortable," she said, bucking into him.

He hissed. "It is, but I'm not ready yet. You're not, either," he said, nibbling on her earlobe as his hands went back up to the dress. Determined to bare her from the top down, he went about distracting her with tongue and teeth, concentrating on her very sensitive earlobe as his fingers slipped between the material and her skin.

For a long moment, he simply enjoyed rocking with her, standing next to the bed, the tease of stripping her as erotic as the feel of her. But he wasn't made of stone and with every whimper and sigh, he grew less patient.

Pulling back, he tugged the elasticized top down inch by slow inch. There was the paler flesh that didn't see as much sun, and oh, God, the slight pink of the edge of her areolas. He held his breath as he stretched the yellow dress down farther, farther, and there they were. Her perfect nipples, already firm and so sweet he couldn't stop himself from bending over and taking one delicious nub in his mouth.

Her gasp wavered as he heard her head go back. Taking full advantage, he sucked, swirled his tongue, flicked the tip until her hands were in his hair, pulling just enough to make things interesting.

After a particularly long moan, he switched things up. Not just to her left breast, but both hands slid underneath the material, up her thighs.

She shivered, tugging at him until he sucked harder, then held the base of her nipple between his teeth while he pointed his tongue, showing her what he planned to do when he had her panties off.

It shouldn't have been possible to get harder, but

when he realized she'd worn a thong he wanted to rip off his jeans before he hurt himself. The tiny little silky number was as easy to remove as a tug. It was the sexiest thing on the planet and she was all his.

He stood up, stared at the wet tips of her breasts. The crumpled silk white thong on the floor. It was incredibly erotic to have her dress pulled down like that, to have the lower half of her covered in sunshine-yellow.

He took off his shirt in record time, toeing his shoes off while he undid his belt and his jeans. His boxer briefs had a dark spot that was growing, and the only thing he could do was get rid of them ASAP.

He debated hitting his knees. Sneaking up under her dress and making her come while she stood inches from the bed. But he wanted to see more than he wanted to imagine.

He lifted her, bride-style, and spread her out on the bed. Ah, his decision had been a good one. Because now he got to flip up the bottom of her dress. "Oh, damn," he said, his voice a hell of a lot rougher than it had been a few minutes ago.

She was the picture of voluptuousness, her hair tousled, her breasts rising and falling, her perfect little bikini lines pointing straight to where he wanted to go.

"You are gorgeous," he murmured.

"You're not so bad yourself."

"It's okay," he said, running his hand up one thigh as he nudged her legs apart with his knees. "You don't have to flatter me. I'm a sure thing."

Her laughter made his cock twitch and his mouth water. Or maybe that was the silk of her flesh, the hint of moisture he could see peeking out from her pink folds.

He hunkered down, inhaling her scent, hard as he'd ever been. Thank God, they had a couple of hours in front of them. He intended to use every last second.

15

CASSIE DIDN'T EVEN TRY to pretend she wasn't staring at John as he drove to her apartment later that day. She'd have just enough time to change clothes and pick up her car before she had to get to work. She'd showered at his place, alone, thank you, because he'd worn her out. She pressed her legs together. God, he'd been an animal. And very clever.

His ploy to divert her attention away from the discussion about his reenlistment had worked like a charm. But he hadn't actually removed her short-term memory. He'd made it very clear, though, that he didn't wish to discuss the issue. Which would have been fine if she hadn't given a damn about him.

Unfortunately for her heart, she did. Even though she'd known from the start this thing between them was nothing more than a fling. Maybe because she knew she wasn't risking forever, the temptation to bring up the topic again wouldn't let her alone.

It would be far simpler to drop it, but she'd be doing him no favors. The odds of him listening to her weren't good, and when measured against the very real possibility that opening her mouth now would end them, it seemed like such a foolish risk.

One she was going to take.

She might just be the only person in his life who could see him objectively. Or full of herself. But what if all his other friends and family could only see him as a pilot, nothing else? What if they bought the pretense that all was well because, God knew, John was excellent at putting on a good front.

It occurred to her that she might be projecting her own issues about Tommy onto him. Different circumstances, but also her inability to be firm with her brother was gnawing away at her soul. She didn't like being a coward. John was a good man. Honorable, considerate. He'd gone the extra mile for her when he'd known very little about her.

Most important, he was in pain. She couldn't walk away from that with a kiss and a smile.

"I'm going to say some things now that you're not going to like," she said. "You can forget them all the moment I step out of the car. That's up to you. But I need to say them because I like you a great deal."

His head listed to the side, and she could see his annoyance in his profile. "I appreciate it, Cassie. I do, but please, don't. I shouldn't have said anything."

"But you did. And I can't let it drop. I know you have a dim view of psychology, but I'm not thinking with my textbooks. I mean this from the heart. A stiff upper lip can only take you so far. I'm sure it's a valuable resource when you're in battle, but the only war you're waging at the moment is the one that's inside you. Your closest friend has had his life turned upside down. You've lost someone who mattered a great deal to you. Both of them mirrored your own life so closely, you can't help but identify down to your DNA."

She frowned. "From what I understand, you have to make a major decision about your future in a matter of days. I can only urge you to go talk to someone. Someone impartial. Someone who might have a different perspective that could shed some new light. Look, maybe you have it all figured out, but I think if you did, the decision wouldn't be tearing you up inside."

His sigh, along with his grip on the steering wheel, told her she'd struck out completely. But at least she'd given it her best shot. She just hoped that would be of comfort when she never saw him again.

"Then again," she said, "maybe all you need is a couple of potted plants in that condo of yours. A goldfish or two might just do the trick."

His smile was tight, and so was her gut. Damn it. Survivor's guilt was never going to be a strong foundation for life-changing decisions.

"Thanks for the input," he said. "I'll certainly take it under advisement. Well, maybe not the goldfish."

She laughed, even as she recognized the dismissal. His timing was perfect, she'd give him that. They pulled up in front of her place a moment later.

He'd gotten over his need to show his manners by jumping out of the car to let her out, and she was kind of sorry about that this time. Instead, he leaned over the console and kissed her. It was tender. And it felt an awful lot like goodbye.

"I'm afraid I won't be able to swing by tonight," he

said as she opened the car door. "I'm meeting a couple of friends for dinner. It'll probably end late."

"Okay," she said. "Have a great time."

"Thanks. Don't work too hard."

She looked at him again, but not for long. She'd prefer other memories to this one. Closing the door, she watched him drive away before she headed inside.

HE'D SWORN he was going to call some friends as soon as he got back to his condo, just so the lie wouldn't keep churning in his gut. But all he seemed capable of doing was holding his cell in one hand, and a cold beer in the other as he stared at some sports event on his big screen.

It was five-thirty. The rest of the night yawned ahead of him in depressing darkness, his mind firmly caught on his upcoming decision.

Cassie had been the perfect distraction, and then he'd gone and blown the whole thing by spilling his guts. At least they'd had that last time in bed. Although maybe if it hadn't been the best sex of his life, it would be easier. The thought of not seeing her again bothered him more than he'd care to admit.

It was the right thing to do, though. She was great, she really was great, but she had her dreams and her job and her own mess to clean up with her brother. Soon, he'd be back on the job, back to his real life. Whatever that turned out to be.

He'd tried to imagine what it would be like not to wear an air force uniform, a flight suit. To never experience Mach 2 again. No more officers' club, no future built around an institution that was more a part of his life than where he lived, what he ate, where he worshiped. Maybe that was exactly what he needed. A whole new window on life. New ports of call. A different standard with entirely unknown goals and achievements.

There were good things about the air force, but the one fact that sat at the top of every list was that it was familiar. Simple. He knew the rules by heart.

The idea that he could change everything by not signing a piece of paper intrigued the hell out of him.

So why was the choice so difficult?

He thought about Cassie again, and he hadn't meant to. But that thing she'd said to him about him living in a bubble. She was right. He didn't have to like it, but he wasn't about to start lying to himself. He'd worked incredibly hard for what he'd accomplished, and continued to bust his ass every single day, but that didn't negate the reality that he was spoiled. He'd grown used to being an elite fighter. He tried not to be a jerk about it, but he'd used it plenty. To get women. To grease the wheels in almost every aspect of his life.

He hit his sister's number on his cell phone and waited for the rings. She picked up on the third.

"Hey, hotshot, what's up?"

"Nothing much. Calling to check in. Make sure you and the family are doing okay."

"We're fine. Are you sure you are?"

"Yeah, of course I am. The last time we talked it had to be quick. So, I'm…calling."

Lauren didn't say anything for a bit, but when she did, it was so loud he had to yank the phone from his ear. Of course she wasn't yelling at him. "Russell Ackerman, you get your behind back in here right this second and clean up that mess you made. Sorry," she said, her voice quieted by half. "Kids."

"Yeah, I know. Another reason I was calling. They're home, I take it?"

"They are, but only for a little while. Russ has soccer and Fisher has hockey and the practices are on either side of town. That is not clean, young man. Do it right."

"I can see you're pretty busy."

"It's okay. I've got a few minutes."

"If I ask you something, will you tell me the truth?"

"I'll try. But remember, I love you, so..."

"So that means you get to lie?"

"Sure it does. Lying is sometimes the most important thing a person can do if they love someone. I don't take it lightly, though, so I think you can count on me. Shoot."

"Is it a giant pain in the butt for you to pay my bills?"

Her hesitation was just long enough for him to know the answer before she spoke. "Not really."

"This can't be one of those kinds of lies, Lauren. Seriously. I can figure out another way."

"Okay. You're right. I miss you, and keeping up with your mail and your bills makes me feel like we're connected, but mostly, it's just another thing on my to-do list."

"Thank you. For all of it. For taking care of me for so long. Why don't you send me what you've got at your earliest convenience?"

"Can I ask what brought this on?"

"Someone suggested that I might have had some difficulties growing up."

Her laugh was like a slice of home. "You have your

moments, but by and large, you're a fantastic man, John. It wouldn't hurt for you to find the right woman. But I promised I wouldn't press you on that."

"And I'm grateful."

"Listen, I've got to run. I'll be home tomorrow, though, between noon and three if you want to talk some more. If you can. I have no clue what your schedule is, but the offer stands."

"Good to know. I'll call if I'm able. Say hey to everyone, and tell the boys to behave. All three of them." He hung up, feeling better and worse. He missed his family a lot. He'd sure get to see them more often if he took Wagner's job offer, but he imagined the conversations might not be so easy. They'd be disappointed in him. Deeply. His father. Man, the colonel would take it as a slap in the face. Would it even be possible to explain his reasoning?

Hell, how could he when John couldn't understand it himself?

He hit speed-dial five, reasonably sure he'd get the answering machine, but lo and behold, his mother picked up.

"Sweetheart. I'm so delighted to hear from you. What's the occasion?"

"Hey, I do not call you guys enough. No occasion, just wanted to say hi. Find out how you two are doing."

"That's wonderful. We're doing fine. Your father's on the nineteenth hole with his buddies, swapping stories and drinking beer. I'm going to an art opening tonight, downtown. It's a fund-raiser for the Air Force Village."

"When's the last time you and Dad had a night out? Just the two of you?"

She hummed a little, the way she always did. He'd figured out years ago that she had no idea. When John had been in high school, it had driven him crazy. Now he liked it. A lot. "Not for a while," she said. "I'll have to do something about that. What an interesting question."

"It's no big deal," he said, before he took a sip of his warming beer. "I know you guys love keeping busy."

"We're used to it, that's for sure. Keeps us young, I think."

"Probably."

"What about you, John? Anything you want to tell me?"

"Nothing new. Sam seems to be adjusting well to his new orders."

"That poor boy. I hope so. You watch him now. Keep calling him, because I've seen some things. It's hard to stop being a warrior when that's all you've ever been. Trust me. And every wife of a retired serviceman."

"Words to live by, Mom. I will call him. I promise. And you, too. Give my best to Dad, okay?"

"I will, honey. We'd sure love to see you."

"When I can, I will. Have fun tonight." He hung up and put the phone down on the couch.

Would he be able to stand not being a warrior? Or would he be strong enough to carve out a new kind of life for himself?

Damn it. He wished things were better between him and Cassie. He could use some of her special brand of distraction tonight.

His cell rang, and for a second he grinned, thinking it was her, but it wasn't. It was Rick. Probably wanting a wingman. What the hell. "Hey, Towlie."

"Devil!" Rick said. Well, yelled. "Get your ass over here, my man. You're on leave, for Christ's sake. Which is why, when you get here, I'm going to make you an offer you can't refuse."

John was pretty sure he could, but at least he wouldn't be sitting here moping. "Where are you, you sad son of a bitch?"

"Me and three ugly-ass pilots are at the Palms. We're eating dinner in fifteen minutes, so move it. We're not waiting on ya."

"Fine. Drag me into sin."

"Dudes," Rick shouted, "Devil's coming. You better pray he hooks up early or none of you are getting any tonight." Then he hung up.

John didn't care. He needed a change of scenery, a different outlook. Hell, maybe these were his last few days of hanging with other pilots. Men he'd flown with. Men he'd take a bullet for. Men who would take one for him.

Oh, yeah. He needed to lighten up.

THIS WAS WHY she didn't date customers. Virtually every person she knew at the bar had asked her where John was. Was he coming in later? Were things okay between them? Did she know if Tommy was gonna be there, too?

Cassie wanted to strangle all of them. Individually or in groups, it didn't matter. Just so long as they shut up about John.

What annoyed her even more was that every time the door opened, her heart leaped. She'd tried to not look, to wait. He'd still be there if she didn't look that first second. But it was no good. She felt like Pavlov's dog, salivating at the bell. Salivating was probably not too far off the mark.

"Tommy said he can't be here until around midnight. He's got a meeting or something." Lisa shook her head as she filled a pitcher from the tap. The place wasn't jammed like the night before, and most of the people there were familiar, if not regulars.

"A meeting. Right."

"I know. But he had a bad night."

"Did he?" Cassie said, washing her millionth glass. "Poor baby."

Lisa gave her a look that was understanding, but also a bit hopeful. "He knows he let you down. He's not feeling too good about himself."

"I'm sure that crackpot lawyer of his will make everything better. Damn it, Lisa, there's help available anytime he wants it."

With a sigh, Lisa put the filled pitcher on the bar, and started another. "Speaking of which, I'm right here. And I know how to listen."

"You need me to explain why I'm annoyed with Tommy?"

"That's not what's bothering you. Okay, so it's partly what's bothering you, but I've seen how you look every time someone opens the door. I won't push, but you have a friendly ear real close by. I'm just saying."

"Everything's fine." Cassie dried her hands, stared at her pruney fingers. "He can't come tonight. He had other plans. That's all. But you know this thing between us, it isn't anything." She shrugged. "I'm just the vacation hookup."

"Oh, you're not going to let that sit there without a fight."

"I'm being serious. We're not an item. For all I know, it's over right now. If not tonight, then it will be in a few days. I knew that from the get-go."

"He worked the bar, Cassie. He called out your brother. In front of a room full of Tommy's friends. That is not a vacation hookup."

She started drying glasses, holding on to words she'd regret. "Let it go, okay?"

"But—"

"Please?"

Lisa nodded, the look of concern one Cassie had seen many times, but never about her. Dropping her towel, she went into the storage room and closed the door, careful not to slam it.

Her face twisted into an ugly cry, but she bit her lower lip to stop it. Kicking a bag of rags helped. A little.

She still wasn't sorry she'd spoken her mind.

Oh, who was she kidding? If she could, she'd go back in time and keep her big mouth shut. She wasn't sure how it was possible, but she cared way too much about John Devlin. The thought of truly never seeing him again made her ache. She'd been so busy flying through her days she hadn't realized he'd become the best part.

Some psychologist she would be, when she couldn't even tell she was falling in love until it was too late.

ON THE FIFTY-FIFTH FLOOR of the Palms hotel, John sipped his twelve-year-old scotch and thought about how he was definitely not in the Gold Strike. He had a panoramic view of the Strip, the outdoor sky deck had glass panels on the floor that were dizzying if one had too much to drink, and the clientele was the cream of the high-living crop.

The guys, all four of them, had been pulling out all the stops for the gorgeous ladies in their finery. Right now, a stunning blonde and a petite brunette were kissing each other, egged on by Rick and most of the men within seeing distance. All John could picture was Cassie. She would have rolled her eyes at the over-the-top displays, the strutting of the peacocks, the alcohol-fueled laughter.

He'd wanted a distraction, but everything reminded him of her. He supposed fifty-five floors wasn't high enough, the Palms wasn't far enough. Which was why he was considering Rick's offer.

Towlie had scored two suites at the Mandarin Oriental Hotel in San Francisco for a couple of nights. He'd lined up a flight for all of them, taking off bright and early in the morning. John's first reaction was hell, no, but the more his thoughts kept spinning, the more appeal the trip had.

He needed to get out of town. Away from his condo, the base, Vegas, Cassie.

Cassie. That would be two nights and three days away from her. She wouldn't even have studying or school to get in the way. The thought of being in bed with her, making love to her from sunset to the break of dawn, was heady and enticing. But she'd become part of the problem.

He couldn't stop hearing her. Imaging her. She'd

taken over his mind. If he got away, he'd be able to think again. Critically, logically.

His cell rang, and he couldn't put his drink down fast enough. He'd go inside, talk to her, maybe spend the rest of the evening at the Gold Strike before he had to catch his flight. But it wasn't Cassie.

It was Sam. This wasn't the first call John hadn't picked up from his friend. But he let this one go to voice mail, too. He couldn't speak to Sam when he was drinking like this. Sam had enough on his plate. He didn't need to worry about John's indecisive mess of a life.

16

JUST BEFORE MIDNIGHT, half the population of north Vegas seemed to want a drink at the Gold Strike. Of course Tommy was nowhere in sight, and Cassie and Lisa were slammed with orders. At least the worst of the nosy questions had eased up, but no matter what she told herself, she couldn't stop her reaction with each new arrival.

"Shove over," Lisa said, pushing Cassie with a bump to her hip. "It's my turn to wash. You pour."

"I was going to cut limes."

"Limes can wait, pitchers can't."

Cassie didn't argue. She staggered two pitchers at a time, careful not to give them too much of a head, then two more followed. Of all people, Spider offered to carry some of the orders to tables, and in return got a free refill of his own.

When the swell of the tide receded enough for Cassie to pull out the limes, she lined up everything around the cutting board and went to work. Her cell phone ringing was most inconvenient, but it could be Tommy. Or John.

Her heart hammered against her chest as she saw

John's name on the screen. "Hey," she said, loudly. "What's up?"

"Sorry to call so late," he said, practically yelling back at her. "I can hear you're still at the bar."

"It sounds like you are, too."

"Yeah," he said. "I, uh, I'm with Rick and a few guys. And, uh…wait a second."

The scrape of a hand over the microphone blurred the sounds behind him, but not enough for her to miss the feminine laughter. Another few seconds went by, and she could hear him speaking but not the words he said. "Sorry. Sorry about that."

He'd been drinking. It was clear in his sibilant phrases, his pauses. The giggly woman. "It's fine." Someone came up to the bar to order a vodka tonic, and Cassie turned her back on him. She should have gone into the supply closet but her left hand was dripping with juice.

"I wanted to tell you," he said, "that I'm gonna be out of town for a few days. It's a thing. With Rick."

At least the churning in her gut made the heavy beating of her heart seem less dramatic. "Oh, yeah?"

"I need to get away for a little bit, that's all. You know. Think things through."

"Sure." Cassie nodded as if he could see her, but she was so glad he couldn't because she had the feeling her eyes would reveal too much. "A couple of days, then?"

"Should do it. Leaving first thing in the morning."

"Okay, then. Um, listen, do you have a ride home?"

"What?"

That laugh had come back, louder this time. Whoever she was, she must be really close. "You need a ride home? It sounds like you shouldn't be driving."

The mixed sounds of her bar and his were a jumble of distraction as she waited for him to say something. To say yes. That he needed her.

"No, thanks," he said. "I've got it covered."

The ambient noise gave her a perfect excuse to get out of the conversation before she did something foolish. He was going away to think. That was all. Maybe some things she'd said had struck home. Maybe not. "I'm getting slammed here. So I'll talk to you later, huh?"

"Yeah," he said.

When nothing immediately followed, Cassie hung up. She shoved her cell in her pocket, and went back to slicing limes, careful not to hurt herself. Not to let it show.

RICK AND THE GUYS were doing something in a bar John couldn't remember the name of. Picking up women was more accurate, but they'd been talking about shooting pool, too. He had left the hotel twice. Once for dinner last night. Once to get coffee this morning. He'd have gone home already but it was marginally better to stare at San Francisco than the Vegas Strip.

Ten a.m. tomorrow morning was the deadline he'd set for himself. He'd make a decision if he had to flip a coin. The indecisiveness was intolerable. For each pro there was a con, for every logical thought, an emotional backlash. He'd even considered asking for a temporary delay, an exception, which was laughable considering.

Tony Wagner hadn't helped matters. He'd called, and when John had told him he hadn't yet come to a final verdict, instead of doing them both a favor and telling John to go to hell, he'd almost doubled the salary, and increased his days off to six weeks a year, which didn't include the days he wasn't flying.

Through it all, though? Cassie. John had latched on to her with the desperation of a man about to fall off a cliff. But she was both balm and curse. Her words kept him from sleeping. Dead of night seemed to be saved for self-awareness and there was no more painful a place to be. When it was light out and he was alone in the suite, that was when she came to him in sense memories and vivid daydreams. He could recall her in such detail it was a little frightening. The sounds she made, the softness of her inner thigh, her hair as it fanned across a pillow. He—

His cell cut into his thoughts. It was Sam. He almost shut it down, but he couldn't. It was Sam. "Hey, buddy."

"Where the hell have you been?"

"I'm sorry. I've been having a weird week. Is everything okay?"

"Yeah, everything's fine, but…"

"What?"

Sam cleared his throat, which meant he was nervous. "Are you avoiding me because you think it's a bad idea? Me calling Emma?"

The non sequitur took John a moment. "No. You thought I wasn't calling because… No. I think it's fine. I hope for both your sakes that she's amenable. You two were friends."

"Okay, then. What do you mean, weird week?"

John smiled. "Just, you know."

"No, I don't, so you'd better fill me in. You always

call back, even if it's to tell me to stop calling. Talk to me, Devil."

John started to waffle, but the idea of being indecisive about one more thing made him want to stab himself in the eye. "I'm not sure I'm going to reenlist."

The silence filled all the empty space there was, until, "Why not?" The question was asked carefully, in a modulated tone. Sam was good at the neutral inquiry, had it down to a science.

"I got another offer. A great deal of money to fly a jet for a very rich man. Everywhere. First class all the way."

There was another sizable pause. "Did someone hit you in the head with a baseball bat? You've never loved anything in life the way you do being a fighter pilot."

John shrugged, although Sam couldn't see it. Thankfully. Because if he could, he'd see the flush that had heated his face. "It's hasn't been the same. I mean, the flying is good. It's great. I love it. I do. It's everything else."

"You're gonna need to be more specific there, ace."

"It's not any one thing. It's the bubble. That we live in. The way we're treated. No. That's not right. The way we expect to be treated. As if we're owed something. That we're special snowflakes and everyone who isn't flying is support personnel, no matter what they—" Shit. "I didn't mean—"

"Okay, no. I get it. I really do. This all boils down to me and Danny."

"What? No, it doesn't. Not everything's about you, you jerk."

"But in this case it is about me. I'm fine, John. I'm fine. Sometimes it hurts like hell that I can't get up there again, but mostly, I'd rather be doing this than any other thing I can think of. The air force is my family. I fit. So do you. So did Danny. And you're not dishonoring him or me by continuing to fly. Life doesn't work that way. It's random, and there's no reason for you to feel any guilt for things you didn't do."

John found himself staring at a spot on the carpet, a well of sadness choking his chest and throat. He couldn't do anything but wait until it passed. Sam didn't rush him.

"She said that I was still grieving."

"Who's she?"

"This woman I've been seeing. Cassie. She's a bartender at a dive out by Lamb. But I'm not sure she's right. I don't think it's grieving, exactly. I do have a new perspective, though. About what's important and what's not. Being a fighter pilot was the only thing I ever considered doing, you know that? It's the only thing my family considered. I was good in science. I had a teacher once who told me she thought I'd be an excellent doctor. I laughed. I just... A fish doesn't know it lives in the water. I've never been out of the pool."

"All right," Sam said. "You've got a point. I'd say, if we were living in a world where they weren't cutting back on fighter pilots, that you should give the private job a try. See what it's like on land. Maybe you should anyway. With your experience, the air force will more than likely take you back if you change your mind."

"But they may not."

"True. Which makes your choice a difficult one."

"Tell me about it. I'm driving myself nuts."

"Just consider one other thing, okay?"

"What?"

"That maybe your dissatisfaction is based on something other than the military."

"Like…?"

"I don't know. Maybe being all *Top Gun* all the time is getting old."

John thought about Rick and the others. How they were spending their days, their nights. Then it occurred to him that they were all still in their twenties. "Huh," he said.

"Let me know what happens. Whatever you decide."

"I will. You call Emma. Don't chicken out. I think she'll be glad to hear from you." John hung up, and for the first time since he'd gone on leave, he didn't separate thoughts of his future from thoughts of Cassie.

THE BAR HAD ONLY been open an hour, and there weren't many people at the tables, or in the back. Not even Gordon and his pack had made it in yet. What was strange, though, was that Tommy had arrived before anyone else.

He was sitting close to the wall, near the silent jukebox. The bar itself had been wiped down, the kegs were full, the stock filled, even the recycling bins had been emptied. Cassie couldn't remember the last time he'd come in to prep the place. He hadn't done much in the bathrooms, or washed the floors, but Lisa had arrived shortly after Cassie, and the two of them tackled the labor-intensive work.

No one said anything, no teasing him about his sudden transformation. But he kept staring at her. Every time she looked up, he seemed to want to say something. Finally, she'd just had it.

She went over to his table, brought them both a couple of tonics and lime. "Okay, I'm here, and I'm all yours."

"I was getting there," he said. "But what I have to say isn't easy for me."

"You may piss me off, but you're still my big brother. So talk. We'll work it out."

He nodded. Shifted in his chair, squeezed his lime until it begged for mercy. "I wasn't here the other night because I was drunk."

"I figured," she said, hoping the discussion would improve soon.

"I was drunk because I was ashamed. You were right about the whole gaming license thing. Len, the lawyer I was hanging with, he wasn't really a lawyer."

Cassie closed her eyes for a moment. It was hard to watch Tommy blush like a kid. Fumble his words.

"He wanted to rope me into a pyramid scheme, and I lost some money. Not everything. I didn't touch the savings."

"I'm glad."

"I don't know," he said, barely meeting her gaze. "I wanted something good to happen. Something big. I've been feeling so useless."

She reached over and touched her brother's hand. Just for a second. "I get that. I do."

"That guy? That air force officer? I wouldn't have yelled at him like that, except I was embarrassed."

"I know."

"Not just about that night, either. I was embarrassed because I was so angry at him for having the life I'd always wanted."

Cassie tried to figure out what he meant, but she couldn't. "What life would that be?"

"I knew you guys thought I was crazy to join the air force. I said it was for school, and it was. But what I didn't say was that I wanted to go to college so I could become an officer. I wanted to be an officer in the air force for my career."

"Tommy, why didn't you say anything?"

"You already thought I was a fool. And when I got hurt, I knew you were right."

"I never thought that," she said.

"Mom and Dad did."

"Yeah, well, they haven't exactly made the best decisions themselves. I'm just so sorry that your dreams fell through."

He sighed. Took a big old swig of tonic. "You got me thinking, though. The bar, it's not the same kind of life or anything, but it's still something. We have a hell of a customer base for a place with no gaming."

She smiled. "We sure do. That has a lot to do with you."

He shrugged. "More to do with you, truth be told. But that's gonna change. Because I want to see you go after your dreams. You'll be a great psychologist. You've got a way with people. Everyone sees that."

She didn't know what to say to him. It was hard to think of dreams coming true when she'd been in so much pain. John hadn't called her in days. He was already back at work, she knew that. She'd figured he'd at least come and say goodbye. Maybe have a beer on the house.

"Why are you crying?"

Cassie touched her cheek. Wiped away the wetness. "I hadn't meant to. I haven't meant to do a lot of things." God, the water works wouldn't stop. She'd tried so hard not to cry. Not to care. It had only been a temporary thing. A few days. It made no sense to be heartbroken like this.

"Talk to me, I'll do my best to listen."

She sniffed. Used her napkin to wipe her face. "I went and did something so stupid, Tommy. I went and fell in love with that stupid flyboy."

"Oh, man. Lisa was right."

"Hmm?"

"She said you were hurting. That if I could put aside my ego for five minutes, I'd see you were in pain. I didn't want to believe her, because you've been so strong. Strong enough for both of us."

"I don't feel very strong," she said. "I haven't been sleeping too well. He never even—"

Tommy had leaned back, was staring straight past her with a question in his eyes.

Cassie turned to find Lisa hovering right by the jukebox. Her friend jerked her head to the right, and Cassie followed the nod.

Standing just inside the doorway, Captain John H. Devlin stood tall, dressed in his sharp blue uniform, his cap underneath his arm. He looked like something out of a recruitment brochure, and for a minute, just the sight of him threatened to undo her, but then she noticed the look on his face wasn't arrogant at all. He looked as if he was hurting.

After he straightened his already stiff back, he approached the table. Stopped just a few feet away. "I'm sorry to interrupt. If this isn't a good time, I can come back tonight."

"What are you doing here?" she asked.

"I'd like to speak to you. But I only have an hour. I didn't want to wait any longer, so I took a chance."

"Go," Tommy said. "Go on. Get. You'll want to hear what the man has to say."

Shaking, hating that John could probably still see the red in her eyes and the tracks of her tears, she stood up. He breathed out as he waited for her to get to his side. Then he touched her elbow and led her into the farthest corner of the bar.

After a quick look to make sure they were really alone, John caught her gaze. "First, I'm sorry I haven't called you. That was me being a coward, and I apologize for my unkindness."

She couldn't speak just yet, but she managed a nod.

"The truth is, I haven't stopped thinking about you for more than ten minutes. Not since we talked at my place. In my car. You made me think. I had to get over myself quite a bit to get there, but after a while, I couldn't deny the truth of your words.

"I've decided to reenlist. The air force is where I belong. They need me, and frankly, I need them. But there are some considerations that need to be addressed. And all of them start with you."

"Me?"

He took her hand in his. "If I do sign up, I've been offered an assignment at Nellis as a test pilot. That means I should be stationed here for a long spell. There are no guarantees, but that's how that program usually plays out. I still might be deployed, there is that to consider, and I can't promise they won't change their minds in a couple of months. But God willing and the creek don't rise, it seems that Vegas will be home for the foreseeable future.

"What matters more than that, though, is that I would do whatever is necessary to make sure you become the kind of therapist you want to be. I'll support you in every way. I know you'll be brilliant at it. From experience.

"I don't want you to change who you are, either. Being a military wife is challenging, but it doesn't mean people can't be happy. That you can't live a life you'd love. Thing is, I want a true partner. Not someone who can throw a great party, although I'm sure you can. What matters to me is that I'd have someone who would always tell me the truth. And who would look to me for the same in return."

He took a deep breath and leaned slightly forward. "If the picture I've painted isn't something you're interested in, well, as I said, I haven't signed the papers yet. I couldn't until I spoke to you."

Cassie was spinning. She felt as if she'd had the air knocked out of her. In a good way. But… "I think you might have missed a few steps there, Captain."

John blinked. Then he seemed to get it. "Oh. I love you. I love you like I never expected to love anyone. That discontent I was feeling, it turns out, it *was* the flying. But not just that. It was everything. I got up in the cockpit this morning, and it wasn't the same as it used to be. It wasn't enough. Because what was missing all this time, was you."

She had to take a minute. Replay each word he'd

said in slow motion, just to be really clear she wasn't making things up. She even touched his arm, the fabric of his uniform as real as the floor beneath her feet. It also took her some time to recognize that the look in his eyes was hope.

"Well, thank goodness you finally got your head clear. Because it turns out I love you right back."

His grin started small, then got much bigger. "You do?"

She nodded. "Despite your disappearing act. I hated that we hadn't said goodbye."

"We don't have to now. That is—"

"No. We don't have to. I think I can do this pilot's wife gig. As long as you're serious about me not hosting too many parties. I'm really tired of serving people drinks."

He put his cap on the closest table, then took both her hands in his and pulled her close. "Thank you," he said. "For being amazing. For loving me, despite my selfishness. I'll try to do better."

"You're pretty fantastic just the way you are."

He kissed her then. Deeply. It went on for quite a while. She barely noticed that the jukebox was playing "At Last."

* * * * *

REQUEST YOUR FREE BOOKS!
2 FREE NOVELS PLUS 2 FREE GIFTS!

red-hot reads!

YES! Please send me 2 FREE Harlequin® Blaze™ novels and my 2 FREE gifts (gifts are worth about $10). After receiving them, if I don't wish to receive any more books, I can return the shipping statement marked "cancel." If I don't cancel, I will receive 4 brand-new novels every month and be billed just $4.74 per book in the U.S. or $4.96 per book in Canada. That's a savings of at least 14% off the cover price. It's quite a bargain. Shipping and handling is just 50¢ per book in the U.S. and 75¢ per book in Canada.* I understand that accepting the 2 free books and gifts places me under no obligation to buy anything. I can always return a shipment and cancel at any time. Even if I never buy another book, the two free books and gifts are mine to keep forever.

150/350 HDN F4WC

Name	(PLEASE PRINT)	
Address		Apt. #
City	State/Prov.	Zip/Postal Code

Signature (if under 18, a parent or guardian must sign)

Mail to the Harlequin® Reader Service:
IN U.S.A.: P.O. Box 1867, Buffalo, NY 14240-1867
IN CANADA: P.O. Box 609, Fort Erie, Ontario L2A 5X3

Want to try two free books from another line?
Call 1-800-873-8635 or visit www.ReaderService.com.

* Terms and prices subject to change without notice. Prices do not include applicable taxes. Sales tax applicable in N.Y. Canadian residents will be charged applicable taxes. Offer not valid in Quebec. This offer is limited to one order per household. Not valid for current subscribers to Harlequin Blaze books. All orders subject to credit approval. Credit or debit balances in a customer's account(s) may be offset by any other outstanding balance owed by or to the customer. Please allow 4 to 6 weeks for delivery. Offer available while quantities last.

Your Privacy—The Harlequin® Reader Service is committed to protecting your privacy. Our Privacy Policy is available online at www.ReaderService.com or upon request from the Harlequin Reader Service.

We make a portion of our mailing list available to reputable third parties that offer products we believe may interest you. If you prefer that we not exchange your name with third parties, or if you wish to clarify or modify your communication preferences, please visit us at www.ReaderService.com/consumerchoice or write to us at Harlequin Reader Service Preference Service, P.O. Box 9062, Buffalo, NY 14269. Include your complete name and address.

HB13R2

SPECIAL EXCERPT FROM

HARLEQUIN

Blaze®

Karen Foley delivers a sexy new
Uniformly Hot! story
Here's a sneak peek at

Free Fall

"So you were, what, just a teenager when you left?" Jack asked.

Maggie tipped her chin up and looked directly at him. "I was almost nineteen. Old enough to be married."

He blanched. "Were you? Married?"

If he was going to be living around here, he would eventually learn the truth. Ten years wasn't nearly enough time for the locals to have forgotten. But there was no way she was going to fill him in on the sordid details. She'd endured enough humiliation at being jilted; the last thing she wanted was this man's pity.

"I came close," she finally said. "But we didn't go through with it."

"So you ran, and you didn't look back."

Maggie looked sharply at him, startled by his astuteness. "My leaving had nothing to do with that," she fibbed. "I simply decided to pursue my dream of becoming a photographer."

"So what about now? Is there someone waiting for you back in Chicago?"

She shook her head. "No. There's nobody like that in Chicago."

"Good."

And just like that, the air between them thrummed with

energy. Jack took a step toward her, and Maggie held her breath. There was something in his expression—something hot and full of promise—that made her heart thump heavily against her ribs, and heat slide beneath her skin. She couldn't remember the last time a man had made her feel so aware of herself as a woman. Reaching out, he traced a finger along her cheek.

"It's getting late. You should go to bed." His voice was low and Maggie thought it sounded strained.

Erotic images of the two of them, naked and entwined beneath her sheets, flashed through her mind.

In three weeks, she would return to Chicago, and the likelihood of ever seeing Jack Callahan again was zero. Did she have the guts to reach out and take what she wanted, knowing she couldn't keep it? She wasn't sure, and suddenly she didn't care.

Turning, she opened the back door to the house, and then looked at Jack. "Why don't you join me?"

Pick up FREE FALL by Karen Foley, available June 19 wherever you buy Harlequin® Blaze® books.

HARLEQUIN®

A *Romance* FOR EVERY MOOD™

Love the Harlequin book you just read?

Your opinion matters.

Review this book on your favorite
book site, review site, blog or your own
social media properties and share
your opinion with other readers!

Be sure to connect with us at:
Harlequin.com/Newsletters
Facebook.com/HarlequinBooks
Twitter.com/HarlequinBooks